Eunuch Park

Eunuch Park

Fifteen Stories of Love and Destruction

Palash Krishna Mehrotra

PENGUIN BOOKS

PENGUIN BOOKS
Published by the Penguin Group
Penguin Books India Pvt. Ltd, 11 Community Centre, Panchsheel Park,
New Delhi 110 017, India
Penguin Group (USA) Inc., 375 Hudson Street, New York, New York 10014, USA
Penguin Group (Canada), 90 Eglinton Avenue East, Suite 700, Toronto,
Ontario, M4P 2Y3, Canada (a division of Pearson Penguin Canada Inc.)
Penguin Books Ltd, 80 Strand, London WC2R 0RL, England
Penguin Ireland, 25 St Stephen's Green, Dublin 2, Ireland
(a division of Penguin Books Ltd)
Penguin Group (Australia), 250 Camberwell Road, Camberwell,
Victoria 3124, Australia (a division of Pearson Australia Group Pty Ltd)
Penguin Group (NZ), 67 Apollo Drive, Rosedale, North Shore 0632, New Zealand
(a division of Pearson New Zealand Ltd)
Penguin Group (South Africa) (Pty) Ltd, 24 Sturdee Avenue, Rosebank,
Johannesburg 2196, South Africa

Penguin Books Ltd, Registered Offices: 80 Strand, London WC2R 0RL, England

First published by Penguin Books India 2009

Copyright © Palash Krishna Mehrotra 2009

10 9 8 7 6 5 4 3 2 1

This is a work of fiction. Names, characters, places and incidents are either the product
of the author's imagination or are used fictitiously, and any resemblance to any actual
person, living or dead, events or locales is entirely coincidental.

ISBN 9780143099925

Typeset in Dante MT by SÜRYA, New Delhi
Printed at Pauls Press, New Delhi

For Amma and Inu

Contents

Dancing with Men

Flair Bartender Robin is rinsing beer glasses when I walk in and take my place at the bar. Robin, or FBR as he calls himself, has spiky hair tinged with red dye, and is of stocky build. He suffers from mood swings—cheerful and helpful one minute, brooding the next. I like to think I am responsible for his cheerfulness at least part of the time. He hands me a bottle of Sandpiper across the counter—wants me to check if it is chilled. I touch it and say I will speak the truth and nothing but the truth. FBR grins and opens the bottle. This is our little joke. It has remained so for the last six months, ever since I first made the wisecrack and he responded.

The three men sitting on the other side of the bar have a problem with the cocktails menu. Their uniforms announce that they are from the coffee shop next door; their body language suggests they have just finished a long shift, that they are probably not going to work another one today. It's not so much that they don't like what's on the list or that some drink is missing. They are confused and want FBR to help. FBR, in his turn, patiently explains the concoctions to them: Long

Island Ice Tea, Bloody Mary, Tom Collins, Piña Colada, Flaming Ferrari. After much deliberation they decide on orders. FBR pours vodka into three greenish-looking glasses, then pulls out a lighter and ignites the drinks one by one. The three men sit on their stools, swallowing fire, their backs ramrod straight, their bodies rigid, their eyes bulging with fear.

At three in the afternoon, The Blue Hawaii is full. The regulars are already there: the four politicians in white kurtas, the chubby girl with short hair who walks like a man and is supposed to fuck for money. A stately Tibetan girl sits in front of a painted background of rising blue waves, drinking what looks like a gin and tonic, smoking a cigarette. The elbow of her cigarette hand rests on the table and she tilts her head slightly each time she blows out smoke. I notice the empty aquariums and ask FBR where all the goldfish went. He says there was something wrong with the power supply the other day—all the fish got electrocuted.

A portly middle-aged woman presides over a table of young girls aged thirteen to sixteen. Every once in a while when the DJ puts on a Bollywood remix of their choice the girls break from the table, two at a time, and hit the floor, their long black hair flailing in the multicoloured light. There is an incredible quantity of food on their table, the sight of which makes me hungry.

By five everyone is gone. The match is over, the stadium empty. The few men who remain pull their chairs closer together as if consoling each other.

Somebody walks up to me and extends his left hand.

'Hey man, I think I know you.'

'How do you know me?'

'I have seen you around, everywhere: Meedo's, Polo Bar, Great Value, Quest, here. Where are you headed after this?'

I say I don't have a clue.

He says, 'Hop on then, we're off to Quest.'

'No girls,' I complain; 'No girls . . .' he replies, 'Yes, no girls . . . so what?'

I turn to Robin and ask for the bill.

'Sure,' says Robin. 'Quest is getting to be dangerous,' he warns me. 'Too many guys, no? They are going to have a fight one of these days. No crowd,' he tells me, 'no crowd.'

I hop on.

It's a black Honda scooter. I sit in the middle. The man in front, the one in the driver's seat, smells of sweat. The one behind me, the one riding pillion, has got his penis adjusted along the upper crack of my backside. I'm going dancing with men.

The sun plays tricks with the sky. The sky is anything but blue.

The men I'm with are men to whom I would ordinarily have nothing to say. They come from business families. Their fathers own motor spare parts shops and television showrooms, deal in wholesale goods.

It's dark inside Quest. It's full of men in their twenties. Everyone is smoking.

There is a lone girl on the floor. She has long silky black hair. Another girl soon joins her.

There is a third girl. She's with her reticent boyfriend.

When the DJ plays her request, she tugs at his sleeve, tries to drag him to the fluorescent edge of the floor. He refuses. She takes the lead each time but succumbs to his hesitance. She does this again and again until she finally succeeds. The men sitting at the bar turn around and watch the couple dance. The boyfriend dances jerkily. He doesn't look happy. His partner sways her hips, thrusts her breasts out, throws her hands up in the air. She seems to be enjoying the attention.

Another couple walks into the bar. They are probably not a day older than fourteen. The boy wears an undersized T-shirt and cargo pants. He seems familiar with the place. They sit at a table close to the DJ's booth, order vodkas and light up. On the table next to them, a man in dark glasses sits nursing a beer. He wears a flowery shirt; his hair is cut short in front, is long at the back. He sits absolutely still. His legs do not shake, his hands do not fidget. The strongest wind will not ruffle his hair. He could be cast in stone.

I see Angelo walk into the bar. Angelo is a tall slim man with long curly hair and opaque eyes. He is a man of many talents. He works as a shop assistant at a music store around the corner from Quest. That's where I met him first.

He would always let me step behind the counter so I could have a better look at the tapes. Angelo is also a dog walker. Often, in the evenings, I see him in Gandhi Park, walking two or three dogs at a time, their leashes wrapped around his wrists. One Valentine's Day, I see Angelo in Paltan Bazaar, a girl on each arm.

Angelo teaches choreography at three local schools. He likes Beyoncé and Justin Timberlake. And it is precisely because he is a choreo teacher that Angelo never dances in discos. He thinks it below the dignity of his craft to dance with lumpen drunk men who wiggle their untrained bodies in completely random fashion in small-town discotheques.

Angelo walks over to my table, his slender fingers wrapped around a rum and coke. He knows about my wife but Angelo is the kind of person who expresses empathy by skirting the issue at hand. He is full of news. He has just bought a new Honda scooter. He shows me the keys, invites me to take it for a ride. I try and feel excited for him, politely refuse his offer. 'I don't drive,' I say, but Angelo refuses to give up. 'Just give me half an hour and I'll teach you how to.'

The place is filling up by now. The awkward couple is long gone. The only two girls there have got lost in the crowd. Angelo and I are talking about the weather when something happens. The music stops. People stop talking to each other. In the dim blue light one can make out two girls holding hands. I can hear screaming: 'They don't know who we are. These bastards. They really don't know anything, Sonalika.' Initially, the girls seem to be targeting their fury at specific people. By the time they leave, they are shouting at the world at large, accusing everyone inside Quest of being monsters and rapists. The men stand in groups, mildly stunned, drinking, smoking, sniggering. The girls leave without a backward glance. The party resumes.

Angelo sees some friends come in. He sticks his right arm up in the air trying to catch their attention. Annie, a diminutive but stocky man of about twenty-five, joins us. Annie is the president of the local degree college. 'You must have seen my name plastered on the boundary wall of almost every house in Dehra Dun,' he says, introducing himself. He has a confident, proprietorial air about him, like this is his chunk of the planet and everyone who enters, enters at his own risk. If you know him and happen to be sitting next to him, like I am tonight, you cannot help but feel safe. We are soon joined at our table by Annie's sidekicks, two Indian Military Academy cadets and two exchange teachers called Tui and Richard. They all seem to know Angelo, who continues to sit facing the entrance, not wanting to miss anybody.

I am not in the mood to talk and am slightly irritated by the crowd Angelo has managed to collect around our table. I came here because I wanted to slink in a corner till the stroke of twelve, the hour when the management turn on the bright fuck-off lights. Except that now, seven garrulous men surround me. They are determined to have a good time, get things off their chest. Every once in a while the strobe light falls on a face in our group. I notice how ugly everyone looks. On the floor, men dance in pairs, their teeth shining like diamonds in the oppressive night.

A sailor joins our table. He's got a girl with him. A dark-skinned girl who wears a big pendant and expensive platinum jewellery. The IMA guys are talking about where they are going to be sent next, may be to an African country on a peace-keeping mission.

Richard and Tui, the exchange teachers, are a trifle shocked at the fact that teachers in their school can beat up kids as and when they want. And, what's more shocking, the kids don't seem to mind, in fact, they seem to expect it. If you don't whip their asses they think you are a fucking wimp.

The place is smoky. The floor is dirty: the floor is all cigarette packets, crushed cigarette ends and burnt out matches.

I go and sit at the bar. I light a cigarette. Two Sikh men to the right of me turn around and raise a protest. I am drunk, so I say, 'You guys look too white to be Sikh.'

'We are Canadian,' they say, 'but we are Sikh. Smoking is not allowed in our religion. Do not smoke here.'

I want to say: Please stuff your religion up your Royal Canadian ass and yes, might as well give it a good shove while you are at it.

I refuse to budge. There is a situation building.

Fortunately this situation is defused by another situation. There is something going on outside the club door. Everyone seems to be trooping out, then trooping back in. It's some kind of fight. The Sikhs are interested. They leave their drinks on the bar and troop out as well. Everyone is fucking trooping except me.

Everyone is now outside checking out the fight. The sailor and his girlfriend are the only ones who have chosen to stay in. I go and join them. 'Typical,' I say, referring to the fight. 'What's typical?' they respond, with identical quizzical expressions.

Something has fallen into the girl's drink. She complains to the waiter. He gets her a new one. The sailor and his girlfriend decide to tell me how they met. Sailor says, 'This time when I got off the ship, I just had one thing on my mind—marriage.'

Sailor girl says in a nasal voice, 'Even I was desperate to get married.' Sailor boy says, 'Thank god I met a girl, this girl—I was so desperate to be married I would have married a goat.'

'Same here,' says the girl.

By now people are coming back into the bar. They resume their conversations. The DJ continues to play Bollywood remixes, Eminem remixes, all kinds of remixes.

The floor is packed. Men arch their backs and throw their hands in the air. The men dance as couples.

I hit the floor and start dancing on my own. I move around trying to penetrate the privacy of these male couples. One of them moves a step back, allowing me to join in. Now there are three of us. The man spreads his legs, throws his head back. I go down on my knees, slide and land under his crotch. My gaping mouth almost kisses the man's bulge. I can smell the smell. I can hear myself singing *Kajra re, kajra re, tere kale, kale naina.*' We reverse roles. The man twirls around like a girl while I thrust my pelvis at him.

The dance floor is absolutely packed. More and more men crowd the floor, clutching cigarettes, drinks, their best mate's hands. A couple enters. They don't look like they are from around here. Everybody turns around and stares. They leave. We get back to dancing. Occasionally, an overenthusiastic dancer loses balance and takes a spill.

Somebody's hand lands on my face, dislodging my spectacles. They go flying through the smoky air. I don't even try to find them. I cannot see anything now. 'Where am I?' I ask my dancing partner, a scrawny guy wearing a blue T-shirt that bears some brand name. *'Tum kahan se aa gaye bhai sahib?'* he replies. There is affection in his voice. I break away from the guy and begin to work the dance floor. I whirl around in circles, stumble and trip. Someone proffers a hand, picks me up. I go to every dancing couple, I walk over to the DJ's cabin. I can hear myself saying: C'mon guys, let's do it. One last time. I am the foreign coach encouraging his boys to go for the kill. We have to win tonight.

And so the night continues—men dancing in perfect harmony. There is some pushing and some shoving, a bit of aggro but not real, more like role-playing. With no girls around, the men have nothing to fight over. We make the best of whatever we have been given: a floor, a DJ, each other.

I don't know where Angelo is. The sailor and his companion have already left. I feel tired and decide to leave. I pay the bill and walk out into the night. What do I see? An autorickshaw, a smiling mongrel, a desiccated jacaranda tree, sewage water flowing in a straight line, squashed Pepsi bottles, cinema hoardings.

I walk up Rajpur Road. After a ten-minute walk I see a sign that says The Blue Hawaii. I walk right in. FBR is still there. The chairs are upside down on the tables. They are about to close. FBR is practising juggling. Cocktail shakers fly around his head in rainbow formation. Occasionally, a hyperactive shaker breaks out of the semi-circular arc and smashes to the floor.

FBR fixes me a gin and tonic with lots of lemon. He thinks this is a good idea. I ask him to put on Guns N' Roses. He says, 'Can't you hear it? It's playing man!' One of the waiters stands on a stool in front of an aquarium. He holds a grimy fishbowl. Slowly, carefully, he puts new, wriggling goldfish back into the colourful but empty tank.

Fit of Rage

I sit on a blue plastic stool outside the Mother Dairy booth in Def Col Market and do nothing. It's the end of another grey and cloudy August day. The monsoon has yielded little rain. Even though it's evening, I'm sweating. The humidity makes me feel like a squeezed sponge.

I should be at home. I really don't know what makes me leave my room. These days I am pushed along by forces not in my control. One day slips into another. Every night is a silent dark space that swallows me whole. I squat inside her belly until she spits me out at dawn, covered in phlegm and bile.

Something happened a year ago. Arpita and I were living in Bombay then. We were locked in the missionary position when, suddenly, she pushed me off. She said, 'Manik, I feel hemmed in. Every day it is the same damn thing. We've been together for five whole years and every night it's the same old shit. No new positions. No nothing. I don't want to spend the rest of my life like this. I feel my youth slipping away from me, Manik.' She sat on the floor and glared at her toes. I smoked a cigarette. I felt deeply humiliated.

Then I did something terrible.

It's not very clear to me what exactly happened. I did what I did in a fit of rage. I remember a kitchen knife, I remember being seized by an uncontrollable urge and doing what had to be done. I recall a pair of dangling headphones playing tinny music.

Defence Colony isn't a completely new place for me. I lived here many years ago, when I was a techie with a dotcom. It was my first job.

In Bombay, I thought to myself: it's all over now, let me return to where I started my adult life. From twenty to thirty has been one long journey. I suppose you could say my life never really took off. Many strange things happened in those ten years. I try not to remember them but very often memories force themselves on my consciousness; they are like stubborn relatives who invite themselves over even when you've made it clear that they are unwelcome.

I have a room on the first floor, directly above the garage. The house faces a school. In the mornings I can hear the bell go off every forty minutes, signalling the end of one period and the start of another. Mid-morning, at around eleven, a drum starts its heavy pounding, most probably a PT class. From my window I can see only a small part of the playground. The ground is dusty and shorn of grass. During the break the girls play a game where they run around holding each other's hands, forming a chain. When the girls stray into the corner of the field visible from my window, I back away or hide behind the curtain. I wouldn't want them to see me.

Defence Colony is a posh Delhi neighbourhood, but in the afternoons it has the air of a small, well-planned town. The roads are narrow and quiet. Guards nap in their plastic chairs, their bottoms squeezed in at odd angles. Mongrel dogs give chase to each other or join the guards in their siesta. A dirty open drain divides the neighbourhood in two halves. Cows graze peacefully on the grass on both sides of the nala. Abandoned bulls forage in overflowing garbage dumps. And cycle rickshaws weave in and out of the lanes, obediently slowing down and pulling to the side in order to give way to passing SUVs.

When I arrived here four months ago in May, it was very hot. I would stay in my room all day long. When the landlady, Mrs Bindra, asked what I did, I told her I was an online journalist. Delhi is a big city. People do all kinds of things. My landlady didn't ask me any more questions.

In the evenings I would go to the C-Block market and walk around in circles. Sometimes, I would hire a cycle rickshaw and ask to be peddled around the various blocks of the neighbourhood. That's how I met Sadiq. It didn't take me long to befriend him. He was a Bihari migrant to Delhi. He hired his rickshaw from a rich man who owned an entire fleet. He was also a smackhead.

Every other day he'd take a bus to Connaught Place and come back with small, innocuous-looking paper pellets. The pudiyas contained the deadly brown powder. He would do it all the time, in all sorts of places. Sadiq had a friend who lived in the Jungpura slums near the railway tracks. He'd go there often. I'd go along, not for the smack but for the ganja which his smack-buddy also dealt in.

When no one was looking, I'd get Sadiq to come up to my room. He always expressed amazement at the fact I lived on my own. 'Don't you get lonely, all by yourself? I just wouldn't be able to handle it.' Sadiq lived in a one-room tenement in Kotla, a poor neighbourhood just around the corner from Def Col. His four children, wife and younger brother all slept in the same room. He wouldn't have been able to afford even that. His younger brother had been lucky to get a job in an electrical repairs shop. When he rented the room he had felt obligated to ask his elder brother if he and his family wanted to move in.

I am sitting in my room with Sadiq and Chottu. Chottu is the newest member of our two-person gang. Now we are a trio.

Chottu works at Mrs Bindra's. He lives in a room on the terrace, surrounded by black Sintex water tanks. His room has a tin roof which heats up during the daytime. He has few possessions, all of which he keeps locked in his grey tin trunk. For furniture he has a bed, a mattress, a surahi, a small rectangular mirror, a noisy table fan. To liven up the walls he's cut out glamorous pictures from *Delhi Times*. Semi-naked Bollywood actresses and foreign models smile and pout at Chottu. At night they go a step further. Some pop out of their frames and climb into bed with him. He says he has felt them touching him in all the right places.

Chottu is from Garwhal. He is fair-skinned, has shiny black eyes and big hands. He is moody and irritable when with us. In front of Mrs Bindra he is subservient and self-effacing, always ready to please. He misses the rain and the mountains, the company of his friends. He's fond of his drink. We do a lot of that sitting in the park opposite the main market or in Sadiq's rickshaw while he peddles us around. Chottu stares at all the fancy women with their oversized sunglasses and opulent cars. He finds it strange that I remain indifferent to the sensual world around us.

We have another hangout—the first floor. The golf-playing Mrs Bindra, wife of the dead Rear Admiral Bindra, owns C-47, Defence Colony. She lives on the ground floor. I'm in the annexe on top of the garage, while Chottu's servant's quarter is on the terrace. Between Mrs Bindra's plush, dark home and the terrace lies a vacant first-floor apartment. A young woman committed suicide here weeks before I moved. No one has been bold enough to rent the place after that incident. Chottu feels her ghost is still around. He describes her as being very sexy, very aloof. She worked for a bank and lived on her own. At night she had boyfriends over. Chottu used to clean her apartment on Sundays. He had a key to the flat. He was the one who found her dead body dangling from an Orient ceiling fan.

The three of us go there sometimes, either in the mornings when Mrs Bindra is out playing golf or when she's out of station, visiting her only daughter in Bombay.

It's one of those weekends. Mrs Bindra is in Worli, visiting her daughter who works for Hewlett-Packard. We have taken over the first floor. The curtains are drawn. The rooms are empty so our voices echo, bounce off the walls. In the vacant space our low voices acquire a rumbling, bass-like quality.

Chottu and I are sitting on a couple of folding chairs. Sadiq is on the floor surrounded by the tools of his drug habit: silver kitchen foil, a new one-rupee coin which he uses as a filter, a mutilated Bisleri bottle serving as a spittoon. I use wax matches to light the foil from underneath while he chases the dragon. Afterwards, he lies down. Every once in a while he gets up and goes to the toilet to puke.

Chottu is drinking. He has finished half a bottle of country liquor and is ranting about his boss. There's too much work. He was initially hired to cook but now does a host of other jobs at the same salary: dusting, cleaning, driving, shopping for groceries, walking the dog, ironing the clothes, driving Mrs Bindra around. She hasn't given him a raise in two years. He says he could kill her. I say I would if I were him. He tells me to watch out; he just might one of these days.

I am smoking thin joints of Stadium ganja. I'm only half listening to Chottu. The more I smoke, the more I think of Arpita. I'm fighting my memories but it's a losing battle.

We are like hikers heading towards a common summit but from different directions. At the moment we are all trekking along on our solitary paths; very soon we'll be united at the summit. We will exchange high fives, shake our fists, plant flags.

At around three in the afternoon I feel like eating. The ganja has made me hungry. Chottu is drunk but steady on his feet. He's willing to join me. Sadiq is lying on the bare floor with his eyes shut. When I poke him he doesn't budge. His clothes are so dirty I can't make out what he's wearing. His body is wrapped in rags. I realize I haven't looked at him much all these months we have been together.

Chottu and I decide to go to Sagar Restaurant in C-Block market. I'm wearing a green Polo T-shirt and faded blue jeans. Chottu's wearing a plain red shirt and dark-brown trousers. The doorman at the restaurant hesitates for a moment, then decides to let us in. He bows and says, 'Please,' pointing towards the windowless ground-floor section. He knows me by face: I eat here almost every other day. Chottu doesn't cast his eyes around the other tables; he stares at the floor and follows me. We sidestep a couple of attendants who are on their knees in the narrow aisle between the tables. They have brushes and dustpans and are cleaning the floor. Not a single crumb will escape their deft hands and keen eyesight.

We make our way to the first floor where a group of Punjabi ladies is playing Bingo: 'Two-saven, twanty-saven, one-zero, Downing Street . . .' Their restless children sit at another table and order ice-cream shakes and kulfis. Some of the women cast suspicious glances at us when we enter.

We sit down at a corner table and place orders for Mysore masala dosas. Chottu leans back and looks around in disgust as if we are sitting amongst mounds of smelly garbage.

After the late lunch, Chottu and I stroll around for a while: Chottu checking out women's feet, I staring vacantly at passers-by. Fortunately, everyone comes to Def Col with their maids in tow so the two of us together don't attract much attention.

We find a cycle rickshaw near Kent's Fast Food. We take

him to the Flyover Market. We need more booze and cigarettes. Chottu is grumpy and disgruntled. He says he can see this life of slavery is not going to go anywhere. He wants money. His present job is not going to earn him that. 'Seven days of non-stop work,' he complains 'and at the end of the month a fuck-all salary. She gives me food and shelter. That's supposed to be enough. Whatever little I have left I send home. I never had any money to spend on myself. I'll never have that.' He wanted a motor scooter but Mrs Bindra refused. Chottu claims it would have made the shopping quicker and easier. 'But no. She insists I do everything on my bicycle. This is no place for bicycles, brother. I am tired of cars honking me out of their way.'

At the Flyover Market I take him to Nirula's for a drink of water. His lips are chapped and dry. He looks dehydrated. He is on his third glass when I notice one of the red-uniformed employees walking towards us. I asked Chottu to hurry. We leave before he can reach us.

We buy whisky from the off-license under the dingy Flyover Market. The sound of the traffic is immediate and loud. Invisible trucks and buses roll past above our heads. We are the small fish scurrying about the ocean floor while the big fish hunt closer to the surface. I buy cigarettes from a man sitting opposite Central Bank. We walk home in silence. Chottu has stopped complaining for the time being. While walking over the small bridge across the nala, I see cows grazing on the grass down below. They look sluggish and bored.

When we get back, Sadiq is awake. He is doing a line. He seems happy to see us. He tries convincing us to join him but neither of us is interested. Then, turning to Chottu, he says, 'So are we doing it tomorrow or not?'

Chottu seems irritated. 'For that you'll have to stay off the brown for a bit, you know. Finishing someone off requires brains and energy. You have neither in the state you're in right now.'

Sadiq tells Chottu not to be deceived by appearances. He says he is ready, that he is an able and strong man—as a boy he fought a cobra with his bare hands; as a young man he fathered no less than four children.

Chottu says, 'Okay, I trust you. We'll need some of that old vigour tomorrow. Not that Mrs Bindra's a cobra, but still . . .'

By evening I had been taken into confidence. Initially I was a little apprehensive, even paranoid. Why were they sharing this with me? Had they stumbled upon something related to my own past? But that was impossible. As far as I knew they had no friends or acquaintances in Bombay. Had the police come snooping around then?

But as they talked amongst themselves I realized it had nothing to do with me: it was all about them and their plans for freedom. They just trusted me. We had been hanging out together for the last few months. They knew our backgrounds were different. Still, I didn't behave like other men of my class; I didn't even seem to know any. Chottu and Sadiq were fully aware that they were the only friends I had. No one came to visit me and I hardly left my room. I suppose a strange kind of desperation bound us together, gave us the illusion of belonging to each other's worlds.

The plan was simple. Mrs Bindra was supposed to return from Bombay the next afternoon. Chottu would go to Palam and pick her up. He would serve her lunch, after which Mrs B would lie down to rest. Sadiq was supposed to arrive around this time and park his rickshaw further down the road. When Mrs B was fast asleep, Chottu would give the all-clear sign to Sadiq. He would then slip in through the open front door; together they would overpower and kill the old lady. They would break open the almirah in her bedroom—that, according to Chottu, was where Mrs B kept all her cash and valuables. They would stuff the booty in two empty bags, get on Sadiq's rickshaw, and head up to the main road to catch a bus to New Delhi Railway Station.

They wanted my opinion. I said the plan sounded okay. They didn't tell me where they were going to go afterwards. I didn't particularly want to know.

Later that evening we went to the Vaishno Dhaba in A-Block market. On the way back we stopped by a construction site. An old house had been pulled down recently and a new one was coming up in its place. The front stood in darkness. The roof had already been laid. A labourer's family was living inside. One could see a faint light in a back room. A transistor radio played film music.

Chottu seemed to know exactly what to do. He took us towards the boundary wall to the left of the house. The ground was uneven and embedded with pieces of broken tiles and shards of glass. Some iron rods were lying next to the wall.

Chottu picked up three. We walked back to the rickshaw, constantly looking over our shoulders, hoping no one had seen us.

Sadiq and I piled into the rickshaw, laying the rods flat on the footrest. Chottu wheeled us to C-47. They asked me if they could store the rods in my room for the night. I had no problem. Still, I was curious, so I asked Chottu why he didn't keep them in his room. He said he would but he didn't want to take any chances. The ironing lady across the road was a bitch. She was always trying to get him into some kind of trouble with Mrs Bindra. She poisoned the old lady's ears with tales. Once she'd told her that each time she was away, Chottu had whores in his room. This had got Mrs Bindra very exercised. She had promptly marched up to his room for an inspection. He had been embarrassed by the pictures on the wall: Mallika Sherawat, kneeling on the ground in a red satin dress; Kareena Kapoor in a white bra and denim micro shorts, a Basque cap on her head. Not finding anyone, she had asked him to take the pictures down. He'd taken them down only to put some of them back up as soon as she left. But the damage was done: Mrs B's ears had been poisoned. Despite her age—she was seventy-six—Mrs B was given to climbing the stairs all the way to the top of the house, especially when she returned from a trip.

Chottu slipped the rods under my bed. He had also procured a kitchen knife which he'd got sharpened at the Kotla market. He went and fetched it from its hiding place in his quarter. I kept it in a drawer in my wardrobe.

After this we said goodbye. Sadiq had to go home. This was probably the last time he was going to see his family.

Chottu returned to his quarter and slipped into bed with one of his sexy, pixelated women.

The next day, Chottu returned from the airport with a very vexed Mrs Bindra. I could hear her complaining about something. I could hear Chottu saying, 'Ji Madam' repeatedly to appease her.

Gradually the sounds died down. Silence returned to C-47. The guards, mongrels and lanes of Def Col returned to their customary afternoon stupor. At around 3 p.m., exactly three hours after Mrs Bindra's return, Chottu knocked on my door. He seemed calm and distant. We didn't greet each other. He brushed past me and gathered the knife and the rods. We didn't exchange many words. He asked me to take care of myself and I asked him to do the same.

I went out on my cramped balcony. Sadiq was standing a little distance from the house, under a neem tree. I saw Chottu step out of the front gate. There wasn't a soul in sight. Even the ironing lady had closed shop, it being time for her siesta. A cuckoo sang doggedly and insistently. A parrot shrieked somewhere.

Chottu signalled to Sadiq. He threw away the bidi he was smoking and began walking towards C-47. I heard them shuffle in quietly. Silence followed. After a minute or two I heard Mrs Bindra's raised voice. She sounded more angry than scared, but then again, I could have been imagining things. Her voice vanished as abruptly as it had started up. The sound of loud hammering followed: the sound of Chottu and Sadiq forcing a lock open.

I stepped back into my room and bolted the door from the inside. Arpita was sitting on my bed, painting her toenails. I had a knife in my hand. I shut my eyes for what seemed like a very long time but it couldn't have been more than a few seconds. I missed her terribly. I desperately wanted to hold her and press my nose into her breasts. I wanted to fall at her feet and suck her freshly polished toes.

I stand by the window overlooking the school playground. It is empty at this hour. Babblers hop about on the ground. They look as busy as ants, pecking at random, immersed in their ceaseless chatter.

After about twenty minutes I catch a glimpse of Chottu and Sadiq walking down the part of the road that curves around the edge of the playground. They are on foot and carrying one bag each. They could be going shopping, getting madam's mixie fixed. Within seconds they have turned the corner and are out of my field of vision.

I know I am never going to see them again. They are going to start anew. I wish I could do the same. Murder has liberated them but trapped me in this horrible prison. They have a plan; I don't.

Yet plan or no plan, things will take their own course. Mrs Bindra's corpse will rot. There will be a smell. The ironing lady will raise an alarm. The police will knock on my door one of these days. I will tell them whatever I know about Chottu. I will give them directions to Sadiq's house in Kotla. Maybe I'll tell them what I did to Arpita.

Pornography

Sunil Singh rode into school on his Luna with very little on his mind. The battered and noisy moped had inspired the boys into nicknaming Singh 'Helicopter'. Some of the boys said 'Good morning, sir' but Singh did not respond. He was a firm believer in 'keeping distance'.

Singh hadn't taught a lesson in days. He spent most of his time reading the papers and chatting in the staffroom. He entered the classroom, but seldom to teach. He'd sit for a few minutes, have some Parle toffees and leave after taking attendance.

He parked his Luna under the big neem tree opposite the middle-school building. It was an unpretentious structure—flat, rectangular and painted yellow. Boys, dressed in their grey-and-white uniforms, had begun to gather in front of the building for morning assembly. Soon the prefects would arrive and the milling crowd would hurriedly organize itself into orderly lines, the short boys in the front, the tall ones at the back.

Singh walked towards the men's staffroom on the first

floor. On the staircase he bumped into his old friend, Awasthi. Awasthi taught maths. Unlike Singh, he taught everyday. He had a hands-off approach to teaching: walk in, open the textbook, start solving sums on the board. He never paused to explain anything. He didn't mind the boys talking amongst themselves while he worked things out on the blackboard. He didn't entertain questions. In the evening they all turned up at his house for extra tuitions. That was when the serious teaching and learning happened.

Singh, a thakur by caste, resented teaching Hindi and Sanskrit in a missionary school. He expressed his discomfort by not reciting the Lord's Prayer during assembly. His son, who studied in the same school, was under strict instructions not to say the prayer. When he protested that this would only serve to get him into trouble, his father told him to lip sync.

During assembly, the women teachers stood on one side, the male members of staff on the other. The two rows formed a right angle with the boys in the middle and the headmaster up front. They said the pledge: 'India is my country and I am proud of its rich and varied heritage', followed by the national anthem and the Lord's Prayer.

A new Hindi teacher had joined the school recently. Miss Das was a portly lady who wore crisp, colourful saris with matching bangles and nail polish. Rumour had it that she was divorced but Singh hadn't been able to confirm this. Today she was wearing an off-white silk sari and a dark brown blouse. The thin white bangles on her wrist tinkled ever so slightly in the silent, sombre pauses which opened up between the prayers and pledges. He had spoken to her once during a staff meeting, but it was a formal exchange about syllabi and lesson plans to which Singh had little to contribute since he didn't teach those forms.

There was an announcement about changes in the timetable. The new timetable came into effect after the break. Teachers were asked to pick up copies of the revised schedule from the school secretary's office.

Singh and Awasthi sat in the staffroom grumbling about the changes. Awasthi wondered why Singh was so worked up since he didn't take any classes in the first place. Singh disliked friends making snide remarks about his teaching habits. After all, he didn't poke fun at Awasthi's couldn't-care-less style which forced boys to turn up at his place for extra coaching. Still, he kept his mouth shut. His son was in Awasthi's class and took tuitions from him.

Singh hated it that Hindi didn't make the grade as an 'important' subject. It was not maths or science or English. No wonder Awasthi drove to school in a car while all Singh possessed was a battered moped. He found the lack of power and importance rankling.

He tried to distract himself by looking at the classroom allotments. He ran his forefinger along a line of small squares and ticked off the relevant ones. All his classes had been moved to the ground floor of the main building. Because of construction work, many of the junior classes had also been temporarily moved into that building.

It was square-shaped with a big open courtyard in the middle. Having marked off his classes, Singh looked to see who was on the floor opposite. Usually it was occupied by the 10th standard but it had been shunted off to a different location to make room for the juniors. As Singh scrutinized the sheet of paper, his grumpiness lessened and the hint of a smile appeared on his face. The floor opposite was going to accommodate the 5th standard. Miss Das taught Hindi to the entire form.

Singh headed towards the neem tree where he had parked his Luna. Puffing on a chhota Goldflake, he tried to picture the future: teaching in facing classrooms meant plenty of opportunities for eye contact. He'd heard that Christian girls were fast but had never really had a chance to test this theory. He hadn't known any Christians before coming here. He had grown up and continued to live in Colonel Ganj, a middle-class Hindu neighbourhood marked by small temples, hole-in-the-wall electrical repair shops, stray cows and a run-down police station. The Christians lived on the other side of town in Muirabad. Brooklyn High School, where he taught, lay somewhere in the middle.

As a boy studying in Government Inter College, he and his friends would often come to Brooklyn to eye the Christian teachers. They were the only women in town who wore skirts. The GIC boys would park their scooters outside and wait for the junior school teachers to emerge from behind the forbidding gates. Most had hired cycle rickshaws waiting for them. When they climbed on to the rickshaws, their skirts rode up, momentarily exposing their thighs. Singh preferred white Anglo legs to the dark-coloured legs of local Christians.

As an adolescent he held a special fondness for Mrs Hamilton's calves which, though not very shapely, were a dazzling, detergent white.

The boys of 9 C were shocked to see Helicopter walk into class on time. This was not part of the plan. This was not the way the world worked. As the days went by, they realized that Singh's return was no accident. He was here to stay. Mercifully, he seemed in no mood to teach. He sat in his chair in a state of permanent distraction, often turning his head in the direction of Miss Das's classroom. 9 C was on to the game in a shot.

Once the boys realized the larger reasons behind Singh's return they were less resentful. They liked the idea of squinty-eyed Helicopter angling for the new babe in town. His laziness, his ugliness, his vaulting ambition, all served to endear him to the boys. It made him one of them.

The location and view had worked out well but there was little progress otherwise. Singh continued to go for strolls outside Miss Das's classroom, hoping for an opportunity to get closer, but none came his way. He'd return, casting a surreptitious glance over her smooth, brown shoulders. He wished Brooklyn had mixed staffrooms. He wished Miss Das wore skirts. He wished they taught the same form so he would have more to say to her.

A small opportunity presented itself one Saturday. It was

the last lesson of the week and the boys in Miss Das's class were getting restless. The noise levels kept rising; there came the sound of a chair crashing and someone shrieking. Singh stood up to get a better view. Miss Das seemed to be on the verge of losing control over her boys. Sensing an opportunity, Singh almost ran towards her classroom. A chalk fight was in progress. Miss Das was standing in the middle of the war zone, pleading, 'Children, I told you before and I'm telling you again: the Good Book says there's a time for everything. There's a time for playing, there's a time for studying . . .'

'What on earth is going on?' Singh boomed, striding into the room. It was as if a blaring television set had suddenly fallen silent because of the power going off. Even Miss Das seemed to jump out of her skin. Singh asked everyone to stand up. The class rose, expectant and nervous. Miss Das moved to the front where Singh stood with his feet apart, his hands folded across his chest. After inspecting the damage for a few seconds, he ordered the boys to pick up every piece of chalk and throw it in the dustbin. The sound of shuffling feet filled the room—the kind of silent shuffling one hears when a group of people enter a dark theatre and the movie's already begun. The only other sounds were those of whispering and the tak-tak of chalk hitting the bin. Everyone went back to their seats and observed Singh with big round eyes. The ten year olds looked nervous, like the audience of an experimental play in which any member of the audience can be called upon by the actors to become a part of the performance.

Singh threatened disciplinary action if he saw any more chalk flying around. The boys made a solemn promise. Miss Das walked out with Mr Singh and thanked him quietly. Singh shrugged his shoulders as if to say 'boys will be boys'. He wanted to look friendly but found himself getting nervous and rigid. When Miss Das smiled he couldn't smile back. Instead, he kept looking at her arms. She felt his eyes on her and immediately pulled her sari around her shoulders, covering them in translucent blue fabric. She said thank you again, this time without smiling, and walked back to her classroom.

Singh had hoped this incident would help break the ice but it didn't. Miss Das remained as taciturn and reserved as before. Singh went back to his routine, which was to sit in class and stare out of the window. Very occasionally, he taught a lesson. Today he was teaching Surdas' verses on Radha and Krishna. He paused when he reached the bit where Radha's tears wet her *cholivastra*: 'I am sure you monkeys know the meaning of "*cholivastra*".' He turned to Jasper, the 9 C triple failure, 'You've been in this class for three long years. I'm sure you know the meaning of this word.' Jasper played him along, 'No, sir, no idea.' Singh pushed his chair back dramatically and glowered at everyone. He gave the translation in slow, measured tones: '"*Cholivastra*" means *blouse* . . . the poet is saying that Radha is so upset at being separated from Krishna that she can't stop her tears from falling. She cries so much her *blouse* gets soaking wet. You have all seen films. You know what happens when the *blouse* is wet.' Then Singh sniggered. This was the signal the boys had been waiting for. They thumped their desks and stomped their feet. A distracted Miss Das, sitting at her desk in the classroom opposite, turned her head to see what the hullabaloo was all about. From where she was, she couldn't see the boys but could see Singh all right: he was leaning back in his chair and grinning at her.

The windows of Miss Das's class had been shut for three days now. She had got a boy to shut it the day Singh's class exploded at the blouse joke. If Singh wanted a glimpse of her now, he couldn't just casually turn his head; he had to walk past her classroom. Miss Das taught other sections on the same floor. She made sure that the windows opening onto Singh's part of the building remained shut each time he had a lesson. This exercised him a great deal. He wasn't sure why she was doing this. He hadn't done or said anything to her.

Awasthi knew that Singh had taken a fancy to Miss Das. He didn't take it too seriously until one day his wife mentioned it to him.

Mrs Awasthi also taught in the same school. She was a class teacher in the junior section. One morning, during a free period, Miss Das complained to Mrs Awasthi, 'That Singh fellow has made a habit of staring at me. He looks at me in a very strange way. I don't like it one bit. He makes me very uncomfortable.' Mrs Awasthi nodded and continued to plough her way through a stack of notebooks. She made a mental note to consult her husband on the subject.

Singh was in a foul mood. Awasthi had just conveyed to him the gossip coming from the junior school's ladies' staffroom. Singh was furious. 'Whore,' he muttered to himself and walked off in the direction of 9 C. The boys stood up and greeted him. Following his long-standing principle, Singh didn't greet them back but perfunctorily gestured to everybody to sit down.

Singh reflexively turned around and looked in the direction of Miss Das's classroom. He hated her for talking about him in public. He found it difficult to sit, so he paced between the rows of boys. It was while walking back to the head of the class that Singh saw the helicopter on the blackboard. The copter sported a big heart with an arrow across its centre.

'Who did this?' he said, turning around. 'Tell me who drew this helicopter.' Silence. He gave a final warning, 'I need to know who did this. Own up and we can talk.'

The boys had been in Brooklyn High for the last nine years. They were too jaded, too world-weary and clever to fall for Singh's let's-be-honest-and-all-will-be-forgiven line. It was a trap best avoided. Their best chance lay in unity. Singh's offer of surrender and reconciliation was greeted with pin-drop silence.

'Everybody stand up on your chairs. And put your hands in the air.' Everybody noisily clambered onto their chairs and obediently raised their hands. 'Jasper, get the cane.'

Jasper stepped down, grateful for the walk and fresh air. Within any school system, freedom and urinating are inextricably linked. He went to the toilet and had a long, hot piss. He then went to the water cooler and drank palmfuls of water. Time was of the essence in these matters. Every second counted. Slowing down the over rate might just help save the match. On his way back, Jasper climbed the staircase one step at a time and walked into the class empty-handed. 'Sir, I looked everywhere but just couldn't find one.'

Singh knew the game only too well. He asked Jasper to get back into position and went out in search of the cane himself. There were still twenty minutes left for the period to end. As soon as he left, the boys burst into giggles, happy in the knowledge they had derailed Singh successfully. 'Poor sod,' said Jasper. 'Dickhead,' said Suri. '*Chutiya saala,*' said Pervez, the master cartoonist. 'No juice in his balls,' offered Monty, the collaborating cartoonist.

The whispering subsided as Singh marched in with a slender cane, taped at both ends to prevent splintering. The boys knew what to do and did it without any fuss and much grace: step down from the chair one at a time, move to the front of the room, bend over a chair, take the strokes without flinching. Following the advice given to him in the staffroom years ago when he had joined, Singh went for the area just below the buttocks. This enabled him to inflict maximum pain with least effort.

Sachdeva was the only boy who created a scene. He giggled, cried, bent over, stood up, bent over again. Singh called for two boys to hold his hands down. 'Sissy,' said someone; 'Chickass,' said another. Jasper was up last, getting two extra for bluffing and insolence.

Singh sat down, exhausted and a little short of breath. He suddenly felt very old—ten years ago he could have caned a hundred boys and not felt a thing. His right arm hurt a little. The class sat in silence. Those angling for prefectship in senior school took out their books and pretended to study. Most just sat and stared into space.

The lesson was almost over when Singh saw Jasper pass something to Pervez. What caught his eye was the flash of colour, like a paradise flycatcher streaking across a drab landscape. In a school of grey uniforms and brown-papered notebooks, the slightest hint of colour stood out like a rainbow. That was how Miss Das had caught Singh's eye in the first place.

He walked towards Pervez for a closer look. 'What did you just put in your bag?'

'Nothing, sir.'

'Stand up when I'm talking to you.'

Pervez stood up.

Singh turned to Jasper. 'What did you just give him?'

'Nothing, sir.'

'You're lying again, you bastard,' said Singh pushing Pervez aside and reaching for his bag under the chair. He opened the buckles and overturned it letting the contents rain on Pervez's head: pencil stubs, a broken ruler, blue Sandoz rubbers, compasses, textbooks, dust balls, small stones, a piece of electrical cord, a rubber band catapult, paper pellets and four issues of *Debonair* magazine.

He asked Pervez to pick up the magazines from the floor. He grabbed hold of both boys by the scruff of their necks and dragged them out of the classroom. He went for Jasper first, pulling him by his hair and slapping him across his face seven or eight or nine times. He extended his hands and locked his fingers tightly around Pervez's ears. 'Scum,' said Singh, 'you chaps are going to send this country to the dogs one day. And I'm not going to let that happen.' He then began to slap him, around the cheeks, on the neck, under his earlobes, on the back of his head, finishing it off with a clenched fist in the middle of the boy's back. Pervez begged for mercy; Singh relented. The bell rang. The boys filed out in silence.

Jasper and Pervez went in to fetch their bags. They emerged a few minutes later, still red-cheeked, their hair dishevelled. Singh asked them to stay back. He let the staircase empty, then invited the two boys to come with him to the canteen. It was a small place, crowded with boys drinking Gold Spot and eating bread pakoras. Few teachers came here. Some boys stood up and offered Singh their table. Word had spread that Helicopter was in a foul mood today. Singh sat down and asked Pervez and Jasper what they wanted to eat. He said, 'Order what you feel like, it's on me today.'

Pervez ordered two Gold Spots, three bread pakoras, four aloo samosas and a plate of chhole bhature. Jasper ordered two mutton burgers, three Thums Ups, two samosas and a bread pakora. Singh didn't order anything but sat with his arms around the boys' shoulders. When they offered to share their food with him, he refused.

Eunuch Park

He sits on a park bench in south Delhi watching a group of old men doing laughing exercises. It is six o'clock in the morning. Today is the first clear day after four straight days of rain.

His girlfriend lives with her parents in an apartment just down the road from the park. He lives and studies in Delhi University, on the other side of town.

On weekends, he takes the Ring Road bus to get to her apartment. He usually stays till evening, has dinner with the family, then leaves. Except that he never actually leaves; he only pretends to leave. He strolls around the neighbourhood till midnight, waits for the family to go to bed. At the appointed hour he slides the latch of the front gate and climbs a steep flight of stairs. She dutifully waits for him on the first floor, the door slightly ajar. He sneaks into her room on tiptoe and they spend the entire night figuring out the basics of lovemaking.

Many years later he will make love to a German girl who will be astonished at his ability to climax in pin-drop silence. If you are one of those who have learnt to make love in hostel rooms where girls are forbidden, in flats crammed with the extended Indian family, if you have learnt to make love in places where you are not supposed to be in the first place, chances are you will be master of the soundless fuck.

He is always careful to leave early in the morning, just before the family—father, mother, sister—wakes up. He comes to this park, reads a book, observes the joggers and laughter club regulars. At around nine he returns to the apartment in a clean T-shirt. He joins the Senguptas for breakfast. After breakfast, the parents usually leave. Sunday is the day they keep aside for shopping and social visits. The sister returns to her den plastered with Marty McFly posters and gets on the phone with a boyfriend in Bombay. Anmol and Roshni take the master bedroom.

Sometimes, in the afternoons, they take an auto rickshaw into town. Once they go to a book fair at Pragati Maidan. Being penniless, they decide to steal books. Anmol gets caught red-handed trying to filch a copy of Émile Durkheim's *The Division of Labour in Society*. He bribes the shop attendant.

Roshni likes watching horror films, sci-fi sagas, fantasy stuff. They watch the Star Wars trilogy at Satyam Cineplex. Anmol is bored out of his skull. Every Sunday, no matter where they are, they have to be back in time for *Xena: Warrior Princess* and *Buffy the Vampire Slayer*.

Making out is a problem. She lives with her parents. His hostel does not allow girls. The art school she attends is walking distance from Mandi House. The art galleries around Mandi House are mostly empty in the afternoons. They spend many hours there, kissing, groping, walking hand in hand.

On certain days she bunks and comes to the university. They go to Kamla Nagar and have vanilla shakes at Chachas. The Delhi School of Economics has a reputation for leaving lovers alone. So they go there and sit on a low wall that runs along a dry nala. One day Anmol pushes his books and bag to one side and snuggles up with Roshni. Under the cover of a register, her hands explore his corduroy crotch. Meanwhile, unnoticed by the lovebirds, the nala has got busy. Street children with coconut fibre for hair, chase each other up and down the length of the drain, playing cops and robbers. Anmol turns around to take his wallet out of his bag only to find it missing. The street kids are nowhere to be seen. He goes with Roshni to the Maurice Nagar police station to register a complaint. The policemen are more interested in Anmol's appearance. They pass comments on the length of his hair. Anmol recognizes one of the policemen present. He had intercepted their cycle rickshaw the other day when they were returning from Kamla Nagar in the evening. 'All you girls from good families,' he had said, pointing a dirty forefinger at Roshni, 'come here and behave like sluts.' He threatened to inform her parents. Her parents didn't know that she often bunked art school and came to the uni. She offered the policeman a hundred rupees, begged him to remain silent.

One day, tired of the lack of privacy, he takes her to Eunuch Park. The park is named after someone distinguished but the students call it Eunuch Park. Men and women of all ages, and all shapes and sizes, go there to get laid. The place has acquired the name because it is run entirely by a gang of efficient eunuchs. For a small fee they guarantee privacy and safety. The cops take a cut from the eunuchs.

They go on a Monday morning. The shrubbery is alive with the sound of bees humming, birds chirping, humans grunting and moaning. They can hear people having sex but cannot see anyone. Every once in a while, Anmol catches a glimpse of a white churidar, a red chunni, a striped shirt. They check out every single shrub in their quest for a vacant slot. There are none. By noon, every bush in the park flaunts an 'occupied' sign.

Anmol and Roshni are about to accept defeat and leave when a eunuch appears in front of them like an apparition. He is very tall, taller than both of them. He is dressed in a pink cotton sari. His hair is made up in a huge bun. He offers to show them the way. They follow meekly. He takes them to a bush that looks like it has been recently vacated. The grass is flat and warm. Big black ants crawl out of invisible holes in the ground. A caterpillar occupies a spot of sunshine on a big heart-shaped leaf. Anmol hands the eunuch a twenty-rupee note. 'Student,' he adds nervously. The eunuch does not ask for more. He sets a time limit—half an hour—then leaves quietly. Roshni pulls up her T-shirt and Anmol buries his face in her breasts.

Someone is calling to them. A second eunuch looms large. He wants money—his share of the pie. 'But I just paid,' protests Anmol. The eunuch sounds irritated, 'Look, I don't know who you've paid but this is my territory. The rates are fixed: fifty rupees for students, hundred for the rest. You get half an hour. That's it. Do it, move it. I don't see the problem.'

The logic is irrefutable. Anmol quietly parts with another fifty. They get back to business. Didn't he-she say 'do it, move it'?

Ten minutes later another eunuch arrives.

Anmol and Roshni have had enough. They dust each other's clothes and prepare to leave. The new eunuch is as serious as the others about his cut. He chases them with curses and threats. But they are on their way out. They do not plan to be back in a hurry. So they give eunuch 3 the cold shoulder.

It's lunchtime. It's time to eat, then return to one's desk job. Anmol observes the love parade filing solemnly out of the park. Everyone looks vaguely familiar. He turns to Roshni, 'Doesn't that man look like the cashier at the campus bank? I have never seen such a look of contentment on his face. And that clean-shaven dude over there—doesn't he sit at window number twelve in the uni's admin section? Isn't that woman over there, the one wearing all that jingly-jangly stuff, the college principal's secretary?'

Anmol is an instinctual rule-follower. He's been like that ever since he was a child. Boys would dare each other to break rules, but Anmol never joined in their rebellion.

There are boys in the hostel who have girls in their room. They have never been caught. The penalty for having a woman in your room is expulsion. Consuming a bottle of beer will fetch you a month-long suspension. Ditto for smoking. Laughing too loudly in the dining hall is frowned upon but tolerated. At most, one might be summoned to the high table and reprimanded. Hungry boys in shorts, and ravenous girls in sleeveless tops can beat it too. The bottom line: dress decently for meals and you shall be served. There are more rules: do not leave your room after ten at night. A register will come to your room at ten. Sign it. If you fail to sign it for two nights straight, the dean will get interested. In winters do not use double-rod heaters or blowers.

Anmol hates being punished. Anmol hates being humiliated. So he follows all the rules scrupulously.

~

One day, Roshni arrives wearing oversized goggles. She looks like she is about to set off down a ski slope any minute. Her lower lip is swollen. Her father suspects she is having sex with Anmol. He punched her face last night.

They go and sit in the college chapel. It is empty and cool and dark. Roshni cannot stop crying. Anmol is helpless with rage. He puts his arms around her, wipes the tears with a handkerchief, kisses her on the nose.

His gesture does not go unnoticed. Varma, the maths professor, often comes to the chapel between classes to gather his thoughts, prepare his next lecture. He finds the staffroom too noisy. He has never taken a day off in his entire working career. He never gets diarrhoea. Today, he walks in to see Anmol planting a kiss on Roshni's nose. He turns around and heads straight for the principal's office.

Anmol and Roshni are summoned by the moustachioed principal. He wants them to sign letters confessing to the crime—Kissing in the Chapel. These will then be sent to their respective parents. The letters are typed and ready. They only have to sign.

'You know we don't encourage public display of affection on campus. We have here people of all ages and backgrounds. You should respect their sentiments. Most students are here to learn. We do not tolerate any indecent behaviour. We will not tolerate outsiders coming and vitiating the atmosphere of this place. What's your name? Roshni? Yes, Roshni, I will send this letter to your college. You can rest assured that I will be in touch with them.'

Roshni disappears for an entire month. She stops attending art school, doesn't answer the phone. Anmol knows the principal's letter has done the job. It's a conspiracy formed by like-minded people—Varma, the principal, Roshni's father—and there is very little he or she can do about it. Then, one hot April afternoon, Anmol is woken from his siesta by the sound of pebbles on the windowpane. Roshni's downstairs in her oversized goggles.

She tells him what he has suspected all along. Her father has turned jailer. She is not allowed out; she cannot make or receive phone calls. Her mother feels he should have done this a long time ago. She is allowed out this month because it is exam time—she has to submit projects, use the college library and studios. Anmol notices that her face has hardened ever so slightly, and that she does not cry anymore.

Roshni comes almost every other day. They avoid the chapel like the plague.

Anmol has two close friends, Nishad and Paritosh. They help him sneak Roshni into the boys' hostel. The procedure is complicated, involves several delicate manoeuvres, and enormous reserves of patience. Roshni arrives at the appointed hour, stands under Anmol's window, calls out to him. Anmol goes down and joins her. They sit on the steps, chatting innocuously. Nishad arrives after five minutes, as planned. He does not sit, but frames himself in the doorway. At times he casually moves back a few steps to the bottom of the staircase, from where he has a clear view of Anmol's room. Paritosh arrives a minute or two later. He enters from the back of the block, takes position outside Anmol's room. He waits for the corridor to empty of people, gives the all-clear sign to Nishad who gives the all-clear sign to Anmol. Anmol scans the outside world one last time for inquisitive eyes and moral custodians, then gives the green signal to Roshni. She swivels around on her haunches, crawls into the hostel on all fours, slips and stumbles up the steps, floats through the wide open doors of J-7 like a disoriented bee.

They finally have a place they can call their own. He can finally play her his favourite compilation tapes. He rewinds Blind Melon's *No rain* and plays it again and again. He spins Gin Blossom's *Hey jealousy* but at very low volume. He loves her glass bangles but she takes them off before entering the hostel. When the two climax, they make sure they come very, very silently.

Every once in a while they have a visitor. Each time there is a knock on the door, they panic. Often it is Richard Lal, Anmol's neighbour, dropping in for a post-lunch spliff. Or a

lonely bachelor teacher who wants Anmol to accompany him
to an embassy screening of a new French film.

At such moments, Roshni quietly slips into the wardrobe
and makes herself comfortable amongst the shirts and ties and
T-shirts. Once, when Anmol opened the wardrobe after seeing
off a particularly stubborn visitor, he found her fast asleep, her
head resting on his blue blazer. She looked so much at peace
with herself that Anmol let her be. He left the panels open to
let in fresh air.

The interruptions, no matter how brief, are still
interruptions. April will draw to a close in a fortnight's time.
Roshni is not sure she is going to be allowed out after her
exams have ended. After much thought, Anmol works out a
new arrangement with Paritosh. He would lock the two in.
The padlock would take care of the casual visitors, leaving the
lovebirds free to fuck and hatch plans for the future.

It is seven o'clock in the evening. Anmol and Roshni sit in a
darkened room, surrounded by beer bottles filled with urine.
Paritosh, who was supposed to turn up at five, is nowhere to
be seen. Anmol has spent the last hour, leaning out of his
window and calling out to people. He's sent countless messages
but there has been no response. Roshni was expected back
home at six. There is going to be trouble, more probing
questions. They curse Paritosh, call him names: 'immature',
'juvenile', 'irresponsible'.

At about half seven, the two are startled by loud knocking
on the door. The knocking halts for a few seconds, then

resumes. They stare at the door, spellbound. Could it be Paritosh trying to tell them that he has lost the key? If that were the case, would he not have slipped a note under the door first?

There is more than one person outside. Hammer blows rain down on the padlock. Realization dawns on the innocents: a pack of wolves is trying to blow their house down.

Anmol knows he has very little time. He pulls out a quilt from under his mattress, spreads it out on the floor. He asks Roshni, still in a state of semi-undress, to lie down in the middle. She does as she is told. He rolls up the quilt, pushes the human bedding under his string cot.

Meanwhile, the group of men outside has been making steady progress. The lock gives way, the inside latch rattles in protest, then slides down in surrender. Four men barge into the room. The dean takes control, 'Somebody put the lights on,' he screams, knocking over a bottle of urine in his excitement. 'Mr Hazarika, will you please check the wardrobe? The curtains, Mr Winston, look behind the curtains.' He occupies the doorway, both feet planted firmly astride, blocking the only avenue for escape.

When the search fails to yield any result, the dean decides it's time he dirtied his hands. He gathers Anmol by the collar and slaps him a few times across the face. 'Where is she?' he screams, shaking him violently. Anmol is too frightened to say anything. He doesn't need to say anything. The dean is on his knees by now, peering under the bed. He contemplates the rolled up quilt for a few seconds as if it is a time bomb waiting to explode, then turns to the warden, Hazarika. 'Pull this out,' he growls, 'pull this out right now.' Hazarika promptly falls to his knees and does as he is told. He sets about his task with the enthusiasm of a boy opening a birthday present. He impatiently pushes the folds aside. The Dean watches on—the proud father.

Roshni looks strangely rested. Abandoned by her mother as a baby, she has spent her growing years wrapped in this bundle. She has floated down many looping rivers, yet, till today, till this very minute, no one has ever found her, bothered her.

The three men crowd around her in a semi-circle, a triumphant look on their faces. They are naturalists who have stumbled upon a specimen of a species long thought to be extinct. Now they cannot contain their excitement.

Roshni lies on her back, naked, gazing up at them. They can't tear their eyes away from her breasts.

But something else, something very strange is taking place. Gradually, with each passing moment, the men's faces have begun to acquire feminine features. They throw their heads back and laugh loudly. Eunuchs dance around Roshni, clap their hands. One of them wields a razor-sharp kitchen knife, its steel blade glinting and gleaming in the night.

'Please,' begs Roshni, 'please don't do this to me. I am not what you think I am.' She shuts her eyes and asks for Anmol.

Nobody Wants to Eat
My Mangoes

Alok was standing on platform 2 of Churchgate station, waiting for his train to arrive. It was three minutes late.

The mid-summer evening was typically humid. Little droplets of sweat covered his forehead, neck and arms, forming a rash of translucent boils. It was rush hour and the station was packed to capacity. Trains arrived and left at regular intervals. Grim-faced Bombayites jumped on, jumped off, stumbled, slipped, ran, grumbled, smiled, sat down on benches sponsored by soft drink companies.

There were young girls in synthetic sleeveless tops, middle-aged businessmen in grey or brown safari suits, plump working women in knee-length skirts, advertising copywriters in meagre ponytails, office-goers in regulation polyester shirt-pant.

What united them all was not language, not drudgery, not the wait for the Borivali Slow or the Andheri Fast, not the copies of *Saamna* or the *Afternoon Dispatch & Courier*, not the dinner at home still waiting to be cooked. It was perspiration. It was almost as if a giant, rude, mean-spirited tidal wave had risen from the Arabian Sea, crawled in through the tiled subways like an octopus and drenched the huddled commuters in a torrent of salt and glue.

Alok's white shirt, now yellowing with wear, stuck to his back like a magnet. In his left hand he carried a striped nylon bag full of leather-bound tomes—he was a law books salesman. Standing next to him, carrying a much larger and heavier bag, was Atmaram—Alok's flunkey and drinking partner. Atmaram was thin, tall—taller than his employer—stoop-shouldered, extremely loyal. 'Sala, no train,' muttered Alok, unbuttoning yet another button on his shirt. Then they both exchanged bags—Atmaram taking charge of the relatively lighter one while Alok held the heavier one with both hands and struggled to balance it somewhere between his middle-aged paunch and his large shiny belt buckle. This exchange of bags took place without the exchange of a single word. It was a reflexive act yet not completely spontaneous and arbitrary like picking one's nose.

In the small space between Alok and Atmaram, on the grey dusty floor of platform 2, stood a small brown box made of packing case wood. The box contained fifty of the finest alphonsos—the best of the season. Alok was going to Vile Parle to see his father and sisters—he himself lived further down the Western line in Malad—and the mangoes were a present for them.

The Borivali Slow arrived three minutes late as announced. But before this happened, before the vacuum train sucked in the dustball crowd, Atmaram, along with several other enterprising Bombayites—especially those who had a long journey to make—had jumped on to the train while it was still in motion. When Alok staggered in later with Atmaram's bag and the box of mangoes he found his flunkey sitting proudly at a window seat. His own leather bag was placed strategically on the seat opposite.

Alok settled his luggage on the long rack that ran above the window and down the entire length of the compartment. The space between the luggage rack and the roof was covered with posters promising cheap, safe abortions and painless electrotherapy for curing depression.

A boy passed by the window selling packets of peanuts. Alok called out and bought two—one for himself and one for Atmaram. It had been a hard day and Alok was glad to be on his way home. The train soon left the bright yellow of Churchgate station and entered the dark patch behind Wankhede stadium. As the stations passed by—Marine Lines, Charni Road, Grant Road—a fitful sleep cast its spell on Alok. And as the train gathered momentum, Alok's head seemed to acquire a life of its own. It swayed from right to left to right, it lolled back and jerked forward; at times, Atmaram—who could never sleep on trains—worried that the head might come unhinged from his master's neck, bounce on the floor once like a football and fly out of the window into the slums that ran alongside the tracks.

Occasionally, Alok would open his eyes for half a second and make a note of the station that had just passed—Lower Parel, Dadar, Khar. Sometimes, these eyes would take in a stretch of road—full of yellow and black cabs, a big cinema hoarding; sometimes he would catch a glimpse of Atmaram munching on his peanuts, and, it was at times like these—in the few conscious moments before the blankness of sleep took over—that Alok would find the city begging for his affection. He would reciprocate generously, doling out love like loose change, and go back to sleep happy in the knowledge that Bombay was Bombay and that he could live nowhere else.

Vile Parle station. As a child this was the first railway station he saw. The trains still looked the same although two new platforms—platforms 5 and 6—had been added to the existing two.

He and Atmaram hurried towards the staircase. It was an instinctive hurry—it wasn't as if they were going to be late for an appointment. Outside there were auto rickshaws, STD booths, cigarette shops, vegetable sellers from Bara Banki and Gorakhpur. The Gurudev down the road, an idli-dosa place right through the 'seventies and the 'eighties, had transformed into a McDonald's. A madman—middle-aged, dusty clothes, no footwear—sometimes shared bench space with Ronald. The guards often had to chase him away. Alok remembered this man from when he was a little boy. In those days he would stand outside the suburban station reciting Shakespeare and asking for spare change. Like a chair left out in the rain and the sun, abandoned to the elements, the man's appearance had acquired a casual fadedness, his limbs and frame a rickety, puppet-like looseness. Every once in a while a storm of boils would wreck his face, the outward manifestation of an inner turmoil. Nowadays he didn't even bother to beg; he recited reams of garble; he was the bogeyman impatient teachers summoned when they had to funnel facts and figures down the throats of their scatterbrained wards: 'This is what you will become if you don't . . .'

There is a beer bar outside Vile Parle station called Namdar. It used to have round wooden tables and dingy lighting. Namdar is still a working-class bar but the interior has changed. Tables and chairs made of moulded plastic have replaced the 'seventies style furniture. There is so much light that you can see inside people's heads.

The décor might have changed but the clientele hasn't. Nobody hangs around here getting plastered. You come here not to lose the plot but to regain your centre, then catch the next train. Alok and Atmaram enter the bar. It's not a straightforward decision. They dilly and they dally. Then they dilly a little bit more. Just a quick beer says Alok and Atmaram finally agrees. They have a policy: no conversation about work after hours, especially over a drink. Alok launches into a complaint: 'My wife, she wants me to earn more. Every evening it's the same thing: *paisa vadhare kamao ne*. I don't think I am doing too badly. I spent two lakhs on my daughter's wedding.' Atmaram sips on his Kingfisher Strong and offers an observation: 'However much you earn, it'll never be enough. And never for your wife. Take that from me. You might be a Birla or a Tata but your wife will never have enough. It's in a woman's nature.'

At this point Disco Daniel walks in. Daniel is from the gaavthan, the local Christian slum. Alok isn't sure what he does to earn a living. 'Alok men, buy me a drink. Today, you staying the night in Parla, no?' says Dan. He and Alok used to gamble like crazy in their college days. Alok was young, bewildered, just about learning how to hang his own little ten-watt bulb under the neon sign of the human race. He'd survived an almost fatal knifing on a local train—the outcome of a gambling debt—and spent a night in the lock-up; had a reasonably successful stint as a mosquito coil salesman; done dumbbells at four in the morning. Dan used to have a Mithun haircut, his favourite movies being *Disco Dancer* and *Dance, Dance*. The echoing refrain of *'Jimmy, Jimmy, aaja, aaja, aaja'* still escapes from his lips before vanishing into a passer-by's ear.

'The slums are gone,' explains Dan, and not for the first time, 'but we hung on. When the developers came with their first offer we refused. Then they offered us a one-room apartment. We refused again. Now, Alokbhai, we are on the fifth floor: two-room flat and a big kitchen. We can look into your kitchen now, Alokbhai.' This is one lesson life has taught Dan: hold your ground and the rest will follow. This is what he tells his school-going son when he complains of pushing in the playground.

In the kitchen there is grumbling. Smooth brown arms that have knuckled dough for years hang still like indolent pendulums, then swing lazily through the air giving emphasis to muttered, almost inaudible, complaints. The sisters are worried and opinionated. 'He seems drunk . . . I want an early night . . . imagine bringing that sidey home . . . that's what happens to men when their wives are bitches.' The whistle of the pressure cooker wobbles like a dying top, then blows admonishing shushes in the direction of the kitchen ceiling.

Since the door is slightly ajar, Alok and Atmaram walk into the house and take their sandals off. Alok stuffs both pairs under the bookshelf to the left of the door, then rings the bell to announce their arrival.

The front room is empty but for his nephew, Umang, who is down from Delhi for his vacations. He is sitting on a makeshift bench made of two chairs facing each other, forcibly locked in a wooden kiss. He is in the middle of a phone conversation about a Jim Morrison song. To his right is a huge double bed. The semi-circular, orange-coloured headrest on the far side resembles the Bombay sun diving into the cool evening sea in rapidly failing light.

Alok's youngest sister, Priyanjali, sits on the bed with her playthings—thumb-sized black bottles with grey plastic lids that once contained reels of camera film; a flimsy little box shaped like a mobile phone, filled with pellets of mint; a dirty hand towel which she shifts from one hand to the other in fixed rhythmic movements. Sometimes she raises her arm and gives the rag a vigorous shake like a cheerleader shaking a pompom. She laughs silently, ceaselessly, her teeth bared like a panting puppy's. There are moments when a frown, a look of horror, crosses her face and she listens with rapt attention to the voices conversing in her head. At these moments she remains absolutely still, not wanting to disturb the precarious

inner balance which seems to have been achieved with great
difficulty and effort.

When she sees Alok, she runs to him. He gathers her up
in a hug. *'Kem cho moti ben,'* he says in mock respect, 'my eldest
and wisest sister.' She wants to know if he has brought any
presents for her. He says he has and produces two small Indian
flags. She seems reasonably pleased with the gift and holds the
flags under the ceiling fan where they flutter half-heartedly.
She stands there, holding the flags, gazing at them intently,
imbuing them with significance, gradually drawing them into
a world of her own making, as those with Down's syndrome
tend to do.

It's kind of dark where Alok and Atmaram sit. They are out in
the small balcony at the back of the flat surrounded by plants,
old newspapers, empty medicine bottles. A lantana bush has
grown wild in the vanaspati containers that double as
flowerpots, rendering the other plants invisible. Here, marooned
on this desolate island, the two men sit amidst the washed-up
debris, drinking steadily. There is little conversation.

The box of mangoes is in the kitchen with the sisters. Alok
is fond of his siblings—Priyanjali, the pompom girl; Umang's
mother, a housewife married to a journalist in Delhi; and
Surabhi, the middle one: married early, widowed early, now
staying at home, looking after Priyanjali and her father. The
father himself lies on a bed watching Rekha dance an item
number on TV. In fact, out in the balcony Alok finds himself
sandwiched between multiple television screens. The windows

of the facing block of flats open out on to Alok's balcony. Rekha dances in every single bedroom. She is wearing an opulent red dress that covers every inch of her. She spins around breathlessly as the tablas and sitars build up to a familiar crescendo; she bows and walks backwards one step at a time, swaying her hips, bringing her right palm, fingers all close together, to her forehead, signalling salaams to a goggled man smoking a cigar. From a distance, it is difficult to say whether the man is good or evil, the hero or the villain.

From where he is sitting, Alok can also see his father lying on a bed that seems to rest on stilts. Beneath him are mattresses, sheets and pillows of varying sizes. They are arranged neatly, horizontally, their disparate shapes coming together to form a solid whole, like something made out of Lego. Right on top, on a maroon bedspread, sits the old man smoking a cigarette and looking straight ahead. He is the captain of his ship, splayed out on the deck, a little frail but still sailing, his vessel propelled by the warm machinery of pillow and blanket. What keeps him going is Rekha's darkened silhouette on the beach— the carrot dangling on the shore and, always, in the end, turning out to be a mirage.

Surabhi has finished her work in the kitchen and is sitting with Alok in the balcony. Atmaram has gone to get cigarettes from the shop at the corner. It's the time just before dinner is taken, a short interval to enable the women to wash their faces and catch their breath. Umang and his mother have decided to sail with the captain for a while, albeit on a much smaller raft—a thin mattress spread on the TV room floor.

It's a hot night, cooled a little by the breeze blowing in from the sea. Surabhi and Alok are exchanging notes about the week gone by. Alok tells her about the rare books he sold in the morning to a rich lawyer. He complains that his wife taunts him all the time—he should earn more, drink less, his children hate him. Alok begins to cry quietly. Surabhi cannot see him in the dark but she can make out that he is crying from his quivering voice and the slurping noises he makes: the sound of air neither inhaled nor exhaled but trapped in the nostrils, being pushed around in circles.

Atmaram has returned with a pack of cigarettes. Alok lights one; the tobacco calms his nerves. Surabhi is excited about her little magazine—a Gujarati journal containing poems, stories and essays by women. She has enough sponsorship, she says, and the second issue should be out in a month's time.

'You should get a proper job,' says Alok, 'what's the point of all this? You do all this once you have a steady income. For how long will I go on sending monthly cheques? My son's growing up . . .'

'But he's your father too,' says Surabhi, her voice rising a little now, jabbing a finger in the direction of the window. 'I spend my nights and days looking after this man, Priyanjali—all the goddamn helpless creatures that inhabit this house. Get a job? he says. I'm sure it's your bloody wife who puts words in your mouth, that infernal stickybeak. And what do you know of art? All you can do is sell godawful law books.' She feels false while finishing the sentence. She gets up and calls for Umang and her sisters, 'Food's ready,' she says to no one in particular. 'Let's eat.'

Alok doesn't want to eat. He says he will eat later. He signals to Atmaram to pour another drink.

Surabhi is sulking. Her sulks are the stuff of legend. There is an insinuating quality to them—they crawl into corners and mingle with dust balls, get lodged in your intestines. This is a especially bad one, drawing everything and everyone who happens to fall in its way into an obliterating vortex. The family sits on the floor on little square aasans and eats out of steel plates with sharp raised edges. There is very little conversation—someone offers someone an extra helping of dal, a polite refusal or acceptance follows; Priyanjali requests Umang to pass the jug of water; Surabhi asks Umang to put the fan on. A Lijjat papad, ridden with bullet holes, takes off in the direction of the kitchen sink; giddy with freedom, it dances crazily in the air, a slave to the fan's rotating blades, before collapsing on the floor in silent resignation.

One by one they troop out and spoon the remains of their plates into the huge plastic bag that is kept in the balcony for this purpose. Alok asks Surabhi to open the crate of mangoes. She doesn't reply. The garbage bag is full by now and she pushes the pile down to make space for her contribution—papery onion skins and empty pea shells, each shell having been cleaned out in a single stroke by the push of her practised thumb.

One by one they pull out their mattresses and pillows and sheets from under the pile on the big bed. Swiftly, furtively, they disassemble the mother ship and find their predetermined slots on the floor. Priyanjali takes the kitchen; Umang and his mother the TV room, at right angles to the big bed. They lie there, sometimes still, sometimes tossing, their engines turned off, bobbing on the shallow waters, an eye kept half open for the occasional inspired shark, an opportunistic pirate.

Alok stumbles around in the darkness, holding his box of mangoes and offering it to whoever he happens to stumble over. In the balcony he squats on the floor, hugging the crate to his chest like a teddy bear. His chin vanishes under the downward curve and pout of his anguished lips; he breaks out into huge convulsive sobs. It's as if an old telegraph machine had suddenly come back to life in a final attempt at communicating an archaic but vital code to the world. '*Mari keri koyi khatu nathi,*' he cries in Gujarati, 'nobody wants to eat my mangoes.' He cracks the crate open and begins flinging the mangoes across the balcony railing. Ripe, red mangoes go flying everywhere like a juggler's performance gone haywire. In a spectacular display of fealty they head down, straight down, past the multicoloured clotheslines and eavesdropping neighbours, to the earth that gave them life. There they lie, smashed and exposed, like members of a suicidal sect. Their guru and his sidekick stand on the edges, surveying the carnage.

Atmaram goes down, picks up the squashed, gooey skins and collects them in a blue plastic bag. But not all mangoes have splintered. There are hardy individuals who have survived the fall with just a thin crack. These he collects in a separate bag, which he will take home with him.

Alok sits on a sofa in his living room in Malad making tender enquiries about the well-being of his wife and son. His wife, Manisha, has made him a glass of nimbupani. She says she had a headache so she didn't eat. Their son is in the next room trying to study. 'Sorry I got late,' explains Alok. 'I went off to my sisters' place. Thought I'd check on them. It had been a few weeks since I went last. And guess what—I took mangoes with me, a whole crate of alphonsos but . . . but they refused to eat them. No one touched my mangoes. Can you believe it?' The memory, just over an hour old, hangs in front of his eyes, taunting him like a red rag.

'Why do you go there?' says Manisha. 'Why do you keep giving them things they will never be grateful for? You're the one who works like a dog while your feeble-minded sisters do nothing but blow it all up.' Alok begins to cry again. He swallows air in big whooping Os—the first unsure tears follow, tailed by a deluge. A powerful booster pump starts up somewhere in the depths of his being and water gushes out in a thick silver stream. There is a hole in the squab on which Alok is sitting; his unconscious left thumb digs deep as far as it can go, and there, curled up like a caterpillar, it rests provisionally.

Alok's son, Ratul, walks into the room. In the last six months he has really shot up and now stands half an inch taller than his father. He is wearing a flowery bush shirt and white shorts with huge front pockets. Alok, still sobbing, makes as if to get up, his right arm extended towards his boy. It looks like he wants him to squeeze it. Ratul grabs hold of the palm, then uses it to push his father right back on to the sofa. With one hand he grabs hold of Alok's close-cropped hair and begins to slap him across the face. Alok's brow has creased over, but he sits there taking the abuse, offering no resistance. He tries to smile but his lips have gone all crooked. 'Ratul,' says his mother in an even voice, 'please get me a glass of water from the kitchen.' He lets go of his father immediately as if he has been waiting all this while for someone to tell him to stop, to exercise his free will, to not be a slave to feverish impulse. 'Just a minute,' he says in a shaking voice, and steps into the toilet. He leaves the door slightly ajar. He emerges a minute later, wipes his hands on a small pink towel hanging in the passageway, goes straight back into his room.

Alok sits on the bed, quiet and expressionless. He finds the lights too bright and wants Manisha to switch some of them off. 'Let me get some water from the fridge first,' she says, going into the kitchen. She returns with a green plastic bottle. She opens a small cabinet built into the wall, just under where the DVD player is kept. Taken by surprise, a baby lizard jumps out blindly and lands on her wrist. She flicks it away almost absent-mindedly. She reaches for the bottles and lays the pills on her hand—two pink ones for the heart, two yellow ones for diabetes, a two-tone vitamin capsule. She reaches for a strip kept on top of a row of bottles and slips in a few sleeping pills. She remains like that for a few seconds, balanced precariously on her haunches, the tablets displayed neatly on her palm like rare coins. They remind her of the colourful badges that Ratul used to collect when he was younger.

Alok is lying down on the couch. 'Can you put out the lights please,' he says once again. 'Only after you've had your medicine,' says Manisha, in a voice that is half cajoling and half threatening. Alok sits up dutifully and takes the pills.

When Alok is done Manisha turns off the lights. She notices that Ratul has left the bathroom light on. He hasn't flushed the toilet either. She pulls the chain, waits for the tank to fill up, pulls it again. A miniature waterfall appears out of nowhere and engulfs the porcelain for a few seconds, before restoring it to its prior sanitized calm.

She goes into the inside room and lies down next to her son. She feels scared in the dark. The last time she felt so scared was in school, when the bell went for Mrs Bakshi's class and she hadn't finished her assignment. At the same time she feels free, as if she is going on vacation. As if tomorrow morning she is going to wake up in a cool hotel room with lime green curtains and a clear view of the hills. But tonight Manisha floats in a world lacking in gravity. She is a weightless astronaut inhabiting a private fragment of time. It is a fragment with no past and no future, the extended split second that will forever elude the constant chasing of clock-hands.

Bloody and the Friendship Club

Bloody was in first year college. His friends called him Bloody because he was fond of the word, using it freely in conversation. For example, if he wanted to watch a film at Priya, if he was unsure about the show timings, if he didn't know how to get back to the university from south Delhi, then Bloody would say, 'It's so bloody far and I am not even sure if they are bloody showing *The Client*. You can't trust these newspapers— always giving the wrong bloody listings. Khanna, do you know what time the bloody afternoon show begins? 2.30 or 3.30? I can never bloody remember. If I go to Arabian Nights after the movie and have chicken then I'll miss the last bloody bus home. What's the bloody point of going that far when you can't even have bloody chicken?'

Bloody was a devotee of bodybuilding. Every morning, in breaks between lectures, Bloody would spend quality time in the college canteen showing off his muscles. In the college hierarchy, the cool students gathered under a banyan tree outside the canteen, the moderately cool frequented the

61

smoking section inside, while the full-on losers took refuge in the white-tiled monstrosity that was the non-smoking zone.

Bloody was studying for a BA in mathematics. No one had quite figured how Bloody had managed to clear his entrance exam, but having overcome that first obstacle, he had immediately run into problems. He found he couldn't handle maths at the higher level. Finding lectures a waste of time he began bunking classes. He failed to meet his attendance requirement and was barred from taking the year-end exams.

But all this happens later. Bloody stopped attending classes for another, more urgent reason. He had fallen in love. Or, to be more accurate, this was the first time a girl had reciprocated his advances.

In the middle of the first year Bloody is still in and out of class and hasn't given up on maths completely. In between lectures he hangs out under the banyan tree, flexing his muscles. The girls are impressed. The girls who are not impressed by muscle flexing are in the non-smoking section, a section that Bloody avoids on most days. Which is odd in a way because Bloody doesn't smoke himself. At night, in the hostel, when he drops by his neighbour's room, it is to read the newspaper and to listen to whatever's playing on the stereo. Bloody, it should be clarified, does not subscribe to any newspaper nor does he possess a music system.

Bloody's neighbour is a tall Naga boy called Viyazo. Every evening, after dinner, a small crowd gathers in Viya's room to smoke pot, drink beer and listen to rock music. Most kids wear their hair long and have passionate arguments about their favourite bands: Guns N' Roses, Soundgarden, Metallica, Alice in Chains, Nirvana. Bloody knows many of the songs but doesn't believe in music the way the others in the room do. He sings along with everyone but is clueless about a band's discography or changes in line-up.

Viya and his gang were in their second year. They had girlfriends and motorcycles; more often than not, the topic of discussion in his hostel room was sex.

'Do you think a girl can get pregnant if she has unprotected sex on the first day of her period?'

'Of course she can. No method is hundred per cent safe. Not even the condom.'

'Oh fuck off. That way nothing's safe.'

'Why would you want to get your cock bloody in the first place?'

'Bastard.'

'Hey guys, just shut up for a bit. Listen to this, man. I had Malini up in my room the other day. We were kissing when I heard a rustling sound. I stopped, looked around. Someone had slipped a note under the door. Man, I was so scared. You know what the note said? "See me when you are done." It was signed by the dean. For a moment I was like, "huh?" That was before I realized it was Khanna's handwriting. Dude, believe me, it wasn't funny. I'm gonna kill that fucker.'

Bloody was a virgin. Not being the bragging or lying sort, he would wait for the conversation to come around to the topic of masturbation, which it invariably did.

Often, the trigger was Naik, a third year chemistry student, who lived in the room right below Viya's. Naik was a teetotaler.

He usually knocked on Viya's door at around midnight with the same plaintive request: 'Hey Viya, do you have a new pondy, man?' More often than not, Viya obliged. The quality of the present depended on his mood. If he was stoned and happy, he'd lovingly dig out a rare Brazilian *Playboy* and if stoned and paranoid, palm off a badly printed copy of *The Human Digest*. Naik didn't really care either way. All in all, he was a good-natured guy, always content with whatever he got, as long as it was for free.

One night Bloody was sitting in Viya's room reading the *Times of India*. Naik had just left, clutching a rolled-up copy of *Playboy* with a Drew Barrymore centrespread—an issue that was much in demand.

After Naik's departure, the conversation veered towards masturbation techniques. Viya insisted there was no right formula. For instance, if time was scarce, say you wanted a five minute, stress-busting quickie before an exam or an interview, it was best to grip the base of the penis and pull the foreskin back rather than rub the entire shaft.

Bloody was usually cautious in company. He was an extremely self-conscious person, always worried he might say something stupid in public. Today, listening to Viya's expert comments, something came over him and he said, 'I don't know about you guys but when I was growing up, I would often use a bolster-sholster. I'd wait for my parents to leave the house, then grab one from the drawing room.'

Everybody in the room cracked up on hearing Bloody's candid confession. It could have been the earnest tone. It could have been the image of fourteen-year-old Bloody riding a bolster like a sledge. Whatever it was, there was pandemonium in the room. Viya laughed so hard his eyes started to water.

Now, Bloody, for all his muscle-building, was a sensitive bloke. Not finding anything funny in what he had said, he marched out of the room, promising never to return.

Bloody was also a man of his word. After the bolster incident, he kept his distance. Since the two were neighbours, they still maintained cordial relations but Bloody never went to Viya's room if he could avoid it.

Bloody had a classmate called Robert. Clean-shaven and god-fearing, Robert was seeing Ashawari, an English (Hons) beauty. They were from the same Calcutta school and were rumoured to have been together for the last four years. Robert had been head boy of his school and was tipped to stand for college elections in his final year. The plan, as Robert never tired of telling his friends, was to become marketing head of a multinational corporation, marry Ashawari and live happily ever after.

But something happened in the middle of the year. Ashawari and Robert broke up. Robert retreated into a shell, spoke very little, took to wearing shiny leather jackets and playing the guitar. Ashawari decided to go the other way. She went public with her grief: Robert was lousy in bed. He only cared about himself. She was tired of his tired face. He was this. He was that.

Bloody had always fancied Ash. She had a glowing complexion, long black hair and shapely legs: she was right up Bloody's alley. One morning, under the banyan tree where the cool people hung out, Bloody and Ashawari fell madly in love.

This was big news on the campus. The college rag, which regularly published chick and stud charts, sat up and took notice. Bloody, who had never made it to the Top 10, was a new entry straight in at no. 2. Ash, who had slipped to no. 8 after her break-up with Robert, regained the no. 1 position. Ash couldn't stop talking about how authoritative Bloody was in bed, the hardness of his abs, the size of his biceps. When Viya asked him what Ash was like in bed, Bloody said, 'Bloody hot and horny, man. Bloody super.'

The Shakespeare Society in college was putting up *As You Like It* that year. Bloody and Ash went for the audition and were selected. Rumours flew thick and fast about nocturnal sex in the classrooms after late-night play practice. Envious Biharis renamed the society Sex Soc. Robert was nowhere to be seen.

The play, when it was staged, was a huge success. Only the first night was a bit of a disaster. The wireless microphones failed. The audience couldn't hear the dialogue. The second night was much better, and the third a smashing success. An old boy walked up to the director and offered sponsorship to take the play to Bombay and Calcutta.

The first stop was Bombay. Bloody and Ash went for walks on Marine Drive, sat on the wall running along Queen's Necklace, their legs dangling above the water. One afternoon, Bloody noticed a number of files strewn on the rocks below. 'I wonder what's in those files. Somebody must have been very pissed off.' Ash felt a little irritated. Here they were, sharing a romantic moment by the sea, and all Bloody could think of was some defeated Bombayite and his files. But she was in love, so she pretended to be interested, 'I know, so sad, ya . . .'

On their last evening in the city, she bought Bloody a pair of cream-coloured shorts from Weekender. Outside Churchgate station, he pulled her close and kissed her on the lips. They stood like that for god knows how long, their foreheads touching, their bodies pressing against each other like in a crowded Bombay local.

They say that in life, sometimes, shit happens. Shit happened to Bloody in the Calcutta metro. Ash turned to him and said, 'Talaq, talaq, talaq.' Well, almost. She turned to him and said, 'I need space, Animesh, please leave me alone. I think I got into this relationship far too early. I'm still wounded. I need time to heal myself.' Then she burst into tears. That was it.

During the last performance of the play that evening, when the spotlight fell on her, Bloody wished the beam would do more—like dissolve Ash then and there, right in front of her home crowd. Later that night, he crept into the girls' wing of the hostel they were staying in. He crawled down the length of the passageway and scratched and whined at Ash's door. There was no response. He wasn't even sure if he was at the right door. A naked bulb glowed dimly, its purplish light imbuing Bloody's face with a devilish aura, making him look more crazed than he actually was.

Once back in college, Bloody burst into Viya's room like a thunderstorm. One kick and he was in. He didn't knock, he didn't wait. He could have been a policeman barging into a gangster's den, except that the people in the den looked more stoned than scared. And Bloody, instead of pulling out an arrest warrant or a gun, pulled out a pair of shorts, whirled it around his head like a lasso, then flung it on the floor in disgust. His voice quivered with rage: 'Guys, Ash and I have split up.' This declaration seemed to tire him instantly. He collapsed into the only vacant chair in the room without uttering another word.

The gang inspected Bloody as if he was an alien offloaded by a passing spaceship. Remember, he had not stepped into this room ever since that fateful bolster night.

But today was different. Bloody got up from his chair. 'Somebody roll me a fucking joint,' he said to nobody in particular. A joint was immediately handed to him. He took a few drags, choked, sputtered and coughed. People offered tips, rubbed his back. Bansal, the hairy jogger, urged him to never stop trying. Tarun, the avid chemist, explained that the roach had the highest THC content. Nikhil, the resident nurse, offered a glass of water. And Viya, the generous host, offered a fresh joint: 'Forget that one, man, try this.'

With so many people backing him, failure was hardly an option. Bloody finally managed to inhale some smoke and, more importantly, keep some in. The dope took effect. Instead of calming him down, it got him all worked up. He said he felt used. He kicked two stools, flung someone's slippers out of the window. He banged his fists on the wall, bringing down a Jimi Hendrix poster. The gang looked at Bloody with new eyes.

He had worked up a decent rage by now and decided to direct it towards the pair of shorts that was still lying unexamined in the centre of the room. 'Ash presented me with these in Bombay,' explained Bloody. 'I bloody well know what to do with them now.' He paused for a few seconds, deciding upon a course of action. 'I'll bloody burn them,' he said, almost screaming. He picked up the offending item of clothing and stormed out of the room. Viya and gang, sensing something was up and not wanting to miss out on their share of fun, trooped out after him and down the gloomy, ill-lit staircase.

Bloody led the small, expectant audience to Rudra Court— a square patch of lawn that lay between two hostel blocks. In the afternoons, the space was hijacked by burly American evangelists who sliced bricks with their bare hands and boasted of personal one-on-ones with Jesus. Tonight, it was time for a demonstration of a different kind. Bloody stood in the middle of the lawn, the shorts held aloft like a Mr Universe trophy, the Clipper in his other hand ready to fire. 'Guys, Ash and I are history,' said Bloody with an air of finality. Without further ado, he set the shorts alight.

Viya's stoned gang stood around Bloody and watched the flames. From the sky, they must have looked like a bunch of peasants taking part in a medieval harvesting ritual. Or a group of courtiers hatching a conspiracy to overthrow a tyrant king. To the chowkidar sitting at Rudra Gate, it just looked terribly fishy and he came charging down the pathway, blowing his whistle, banging his stick on the ground. The racket he was making gave the group enough time to flee. The chowkidar contemplated the half-burnt shorts, then set off in the direction of the principal's residence, the lathi tucked under his armpit like an umbrella.

Bloody lay in his bed, listlessly playing with a sealed envelope. His eyes though were somewhere else. They were focussed on two fat brown lizards out hunting on the room's ceiling. They would stalk out prey—a tiny winged insect or dull-coloured, restful moths—then lie in wait patiently. Choosing the right moment, the mini-beast slithered in for the kill, deftly trapping the clueless bug in its miniature jaws. It then sat there, not blinking, not moving, sucking the insect dry in an efficient manoeuvre Bloody liked to call the Terminal Munch.

After a while, Bloody tired of the lizards and turned his attention to the white envelope in his hand. On certain days of the week, the newspapers carried small, boxed ads for friendship clubs. The advertisements featured three or four numbers printed over a blonde's smiling face. One of the first things he'd done on his return from Calcutta that morning was to call one of these numbers.

An hour after he placed the call, a portly gentleman arrived at his door and handed him an envelope that bore the legend: Interlink Friendship Service. Bloody gave the man one thousand rupees. The man gave him the envelope and left.

Bloody had not opened the envelope all day. He turned it around in his hands over and over again. He tore a corner of the envelope, inserted his finger into the tiny cavity and ripped the top open. The plain white sheet of paper inside listed details of five potential women-friends:

NAME	AGE	OCCUPATION	HOBBIES
Sunita	26	Working	Internet chatting, watching movies
Dipti	19	Student	Watching movies, shopping, dancing

NAME	AGE	OCCUPATION	HOBBIES
Sudha	35	Housewife	Travelling, watching TV
Priya	28	Working	Shopping, movies, eating out, painting
Dolly	20	Student	Watching cricket, listening to music, talking to friends

Bloody turned on the table lamp and sat at his desk. He looked like he was going to embark on a self-inflicted mock test. He uncapped his pen and, like a father encircling suitable brides for his son in the Sunday matrimonials, ticked two names.

At first, he tried calling Dipti and Dolly. In each case, a recorded message informed him that the number he had dialled did not exist. With a sinking heart, he tried Priya. Her phone was switched off. It was down to the final two. Sudha, or someone claiming to be her, picked up the phone. Bloody heard babies squalling in the background. Yes, said Sudha, she was part of the friendship club network, except that these days she was very busy. The children were not keeping well. Besides, her sister was visiting for a few days. Would he mind calling later, please? His frustration mounting, Bloody called Sunita's number. A man claiming to be a panwala answered the call. Yes, a girl by the name of Sunita had rented the phone for the day but it was now back in the shop. Bloody had never heard of a panwala running a mobile phone renting service. None of the numbers worked. This was daylight robbery. Not wanting to accept defeat so easily, he called the original number, the one in the ad. A woman picked up. Her voice sounded familiar. He had spoken to her in the morning.

Bloody decided to give her a piece of his mind: 'Listen,' he shouted, 'I hope you remember me because this morning I had called your bloody friendship club but none of the bloody numbers seem to work. There is no Dipti and no bloody Dolly. You bloody well give me numbers that work or I want my bloody money back.'

The lady at the other end heard him out patiently, then said, 'So sorry. Wrong number.' She then cut the line. Bloody tried calling her number many times but only got an engaged tone.

It had been a long and tiring day. Still, he couldn't sleep. At around two in the morning, Bloody decided there was no point lying around in bed. He switched on the lights, got dressed and walked across to Viya's block. The party was still on, though everyone looked more subdued than earlier. While the joints had stopped going around, other items were still in circulation: a bottle of ice-cold water, a Mars bar, a bottle of Visine eye drops.

The action, though, lay in the centre of the room, at the very spot, where just a few hours earlier, Bloody had deposited a pair of Weekender shorts. Viya squatted on the floor, lizard in hand, trying to stuff its mouth with chewing tobacco. As soon as he managed to get a small quantity in, he tied its mouth with a piece of string and let it go. Dizzy with baccy juice, the lizard leaped around doing back flips, like a gasping fish left on the beach by a receding wave. Two lizards lay inert on the floor, exhausted, comatose or maybe even dead. Viya turned around and warned his mesmerized audience: 'Guys, we are running out of lizards.'

Bloody suddenly remembered the two fat ones on his ceiling. 'Viya, I think there are a couple in my room. I'll go get them. Can you pass me that little box please?'

'Oh great,' said Viya, rising from his haunches and looking for his slippers. 'Hold on a sec, man. I'll come with you.'

Rubber Band

This had come up before. On Sunday night I cornered her for the seventy-seventh time. I don't trust you, I said, I still don't trust you. Did he kiss you? How far did it go? Why didn't you push him away right in the beginning?

She cried, she screamed. She said she'd slept with 10,000 men. She said *he* was a nice man. Then she had one of her seizures. I lay her down on the couch in the lateral position. I wiped her foaming lips a couple of times before lighting up a cigarette.

The first time she had a fit, we were in a seedy hotel room in Paharganj. I was in New Delhi for a job interview.

It had been a mixed day. We started with a beer breakfast at the United Coffee House. We made love in the afternoon, then stepped out for lunch.

She ate her special thali without any joy. But I made you come three times in a row, I protested. Aren't you happy? No, said Madhu, curling her tongue over her upper lip, you are an unsettling influence on my life.

Back in the hotel room she complained of tiredness. She

74

sat down on the double bed and cleaned her nails with a file. She then lay down on her back and shut her eyes.

The room was in a mess. I set about tidying up; her stringy tops and chunnis, the discarded condoms on the floor—the semen attracting a train of ants like stale lemonade. Big black ants arrived, sniffed, then moved away.

I have been tidying up for the past twenty minutes. I have completely forgotten about Madhu. When I look up I see her eyes quivering. I smile. I say, nice one, Madhu. The quivering doesn't stop. I drop the broom and rush to the bed. Stop joking, Madhu. She bangs her fists on the bed, her entire body overcome by convulsions. Her full lips and dainty chin have disappeared under a river of spittle; her mouth is a frothing volcano.

For the first time I scream. Madhoooo . . . you can't do this . . . come back . . . don't die on me. My scream runs down the corridor and returns chastened, a trifle muted. I lift her head and wipe the spit with a mauve towelling napkin my mother bought for me in Bombay. I know she is going to die. I think of the seedy hotel room. I think of Delhi cops. I think about the status of unmarried couples in India. I am thinking of jail when the convulsions cease.

That evening, it happens for the second time. We are standing opposite Sagar in Defence Colony market. We are supposed to meet my photographer friend Prashant. Def Col is crawling with Def Col women. Tight jeans, sleeveless tops, manicured nails, long straight hair. I follow one specimen with my eyes. She enters a grocery store and emerges with a tube of Pringles. I fumble in my trouser pocket for a broken cigarette.

I notice that people are looking at me. In fact they seem to be looking at my shoes. I look at my shoes. Madhu has fallen on the road. She is banging her fists again. Electricity courses through her veins. We are surrounded by people. My cigarette rolls towards someone's pink toenails packed tight in stiletto heels. Car wheels pass inches from her hair, her head. Somebody gets me a bottle of mineral water. I splash some on her face. I hear myself screaming.

When she comes to she has no eyeballs. I look into the blank white spaces under her eyelids. Her cheeks are streaked with eyeliner. People lean out of their cars and stare at us with hungry eyes. There is a caterer's shop across the road. The owner walks across and invites us in. The shop has a bed; he suggests she can lie down there.

Madhu's head is on my right thigh. I am stroking her hair with my right hand. My other hand is trying to tidy up. The contents of her handbag are all over the road. An eyeshadow pencil. A strip of Alprax. A Nokia phone. A black Reynolds ballpoint. One loose morning-after pill lying millimetres from a cake of cow dung.

I call Prashant from her Nokia. Prashant, man, where are you? This is an emergency. Hurry.

Dude, says Prashant's distorted voice, I'm stuck in a traffic jam near Ansal Plaza.

In the shop everything is white: the tablecloths, the cups and saucers, the porcelain plates. She opens her eyes. The eyeballs are back. She is clutching the purple hanky. She smiles a weak smile and says she loves me. I realize for the first time that I am in love with her. Where am I, she says, and what happened?

━━━╱━━━

Where am I, she says, and what happened? She is lying on the couch. I am sitting on the floor, by her feet.

You had another seizure.

You know my weak spots and you hit me there. You are cruel. So what if I slept with that man? Even if I did—and I did not—what about all the love I have given you?

I say I am going to call her doctor. I can picture the neurologist: small, bald, owl-like eyes, a messiah from another planet.

Do you like doing this to me?

I find myself getting angry. I can't think straight. I find myself shouting at her: You can't stop me from asking questions. I want answers. I want a simple life.

━━━╱━━━

That night we sleep separately. At 3 I get up and go to the bedroom. She is half-asleep, trying to sleep.

I think about tomorrow. She will be nervous, irritable, hypersensitive. She will have memory lapses, her brain will fizz and pop. She will remember things I said five years ago.

Without realizing it I have begun pacing the room. My feet leave marks on the dusty floor. These marks mingle with other marks from the past—the wet bathroom slippers from

Sunday morning, the big, flying cockroach I crushed yesterday afternoon.

I turn my head and look at her. I love her when she is asleep. The only other time I love her this much is just after she's had a seizure and she's lying there, her body inert, the eyeballs missing. At that moment all I want to do is dive into the white spaces underneath her eyelids and hit rock bottom.

I walk out on to our first floor balcony and spend half an hour drumming my fingers on the rickety wooden railing. When I stop, I notice that the night smells of leather and that the plants need watering.

Okhla Basti

Angad, twenty-six years old, of medium build and receding hairline, a middle-level techie in a sinking dot com, walked down the narrow path that dipped steeply, spread out into a modest valley, before rising up again into a second mound.

Children ran up and down the slopes like mountain goats. A stream of water came trickling down to meet the giant puddle at the bottom of the second mound, the one Angad had just begun to ascend.

Nasir bhai's smoking den was situated right on top, like a sentry box outside a fortress town. Beyond, the slum spread out like a labyrinth—a mottle of brown and black—as far as the eye could see.

Angad often wondered what he was doing in a place like this—a place far removed from his own world, the world he was born into and worked in, one with whose rules he bore an instinctive familiarity. Could it be that failing to understand its rules, he was looking for a different world, with different rules?

In the basti, no one seemed to grudge his presence, or particularly care who he was, what name he went under, what job he did. They didn't ask why he stayed on when others of his kind came, picked up stuff and left as soon as possible. It was also probably easier to be accepted in a community which was made of a refugee people in the first place; uprooted from Bangladesh, now living in a squalid slum in New Delhi, they knew the feeling of being on the run, knew the value of temporary resting places.

Two hours later, the sun had set and Angad lay stoned on a thick wooden plank. Around him the basti thrummed with evening activity. The men, back after a hard day's labour, assembled around Nasir bhai's shop for their ten-rupee fix of cheap weed; those of a more gregarious disposition sauntered down the narrow path that divided the basti into two halves to Gopal's shack where they would buy sachets of spiced country liquor. The women, their saris hitched up to their knees, carried pails of water for cooking and bathing. From where Angad lay he could see their bare legs—the calves all muscular and polka-dotted with mud—walk past him briskly, until they disappeared behind the opaque smoke of coal fires. Children in faded rags, some wearing nothing, ran around screaming, shouting, creating confusion. Every once in a while, when a pheriwala arrived selling candyfloss or blow-bubble toys, the children's clamour reached a new crescendo.

Mullaji was back in his butcher's shop for evening duty. A bewildered chicken escaped from the makeshift slab just as he was about to slaughter it, and scrambled down the basti, its wings scraping Angad's nose. Mullaji cursed before taking off in weary pursuit. This was the fourth time in two days that the chicken had escaped execution. You knew Mullaji's patience was at the end of its tether when the vein under the dagger-shaped scar on his back turned a peculiar shade of purple.

On a normal day, Angad did not hang around the slum for this long. Today was unusual—Ilyas was expected back from his village after a three-month vacation. No one was sure whether he had gone on holiday or business. Often the thought crossed Angad's mind that Ilyas was behind bars and the 'gone to his village' bit was just a story concocted to satisfy his curiosity.

Ilyas was the only person Angad was kind of close to in the slum. He spoke to the others, listened patiently to their tales of tragedy and bravado; in fact, one could say Angad was reasonably popular in Okhla Basti, but it was with Ilyas he felt some kind of affinity. They had met—as most relationships in Okhla Basti began—over a chillum at Nasir bhai's. Though not new to the slum—he had been living there for the last ten years—Illyas was new to the ganja trade. He had spent the better part of the decade selling vegetables at the wholesale market attached to the slum. That gave him status and prestige in a basti where the predominant occupations were rickshaw-pulling and refuse collection. In the narrow strip of land between Nasir bhai's shop and the vegetable mandi, families gathered in groups, painstakingly sorting out the garbage the city had vomited. Glass was separated from plastic, rubber from metal, dirty syringes from bloodstained cotton wool.

Ilyas, who was getting jaded selling cauliflower, had been brought in by the enterprising and eagle-eyed Nasir bhai as a replacement for Tinku, his right-hand man. Tinku had a fondness for fishnet singlets and imitation gold necklaces. Thin as a stick, he liked talking big. He would tamper with the measuring scale and get into scraps with customers, thereby attracting unnecessary attention to Nasir bhai's shop. Once, on an impulse—an impulse Angad regretted later—he had taken Tinku home with him, and then out for dinner. Later, he had found some cash missing from his cupboard; he was convinced Tinku had stolen the money. It so happened that Nasir bhai decided to sack Tinku at around the same time Angad had taken him home. He disappeared from the slum that very night after threatening to burn down the entire basti. As Mullaji, who was witness to the entire incident, recalled later, 'The rage in the boy's eyes was enough; he would have required neither kerosene nor matchstick.'

When Ilyas finally arrived it was eight. Angad scrutinized him for signs of a prison stint but could not tell. He had shaved and looked like he had been eating well. A blue denim shirt hung loose over his brown terrycot trousers. As soon as Ilyas saw Angad, he broke through the circle of people who had surrounded him on his arrival and walked across. They hugged, then Ilyas drew back, his hands resting on Angad's shoulders. 'Good to see you, boss,' he said. Angad smiled and said, 'Ilyas bhai, my good friend,' and then fell silent. 'So, how was the trip to the village?' asked Angad. 'Not too bad,' replied Ilyas, 'not too bad at all.' They never had much to say to each other. Still, Angad always felt happy to see Ilyas and today was no different. Somehow the shyness, the awkwardness, the lack of conversation didn't seem to affect their friendship much.

'I hope you're staying back for a while today,' said Ilyas, his eyes doing a 360-degree scan, acknowledging greetings, taking in the changes that had crept in while he was away.

Angad checked the time. Light from a naked 100-watt electric bulb streamed out of a tiny window in Nasir bhai's smoking den and bounced off the steel strap of his Titan watch, split into a hundred tiny bullets. 'Let's take it as it comes,' said Angad, 'but I should leave before it gets too late.'

The time was half past ten. A cold wind cut through Okhla Basti, chilling its sparsely clad residents to the bone. Angad, Ilyas, Mullaji, Nasir bhai and a few others sat around a bonfire, talking.

The slum had seen a fire recently. Nobody died but most people had lost whatever little they owned—an aluminium pan, a tin trunk, meagre savings stashed away in an empty Hajmola bottle. Someone said they would all be packed off to Narela soon.

A balding, oily faced man asked Angad to drink a spoon of ghee dissolved in water when he went back home. 'That'll keep your lungs going for years,' he advised with the confidence of a veteran. Mullaji bragged about his various businesses and the excellent condition of his body after forty-eight years and seven daughters, as if he had given birth to them himself. Dheeraj, one of Nasir bhai's junior employees, spoke of someone in his village who got so addicted to the chillum that he just sat stoned on his bed all the time. 'He was a landed man,' said Dheeraj, 'but everything is gone now and he doesn't care.'

It was 25 January. Usually Nasir bhai kept the den open till late. He would go back to his wife and children, not being much of a smoker himself, leaving Ilyas with the responsibility of shutting the place around midnight.

With Republic Day approaching, the police had been uncharacteristically strict. They wanted the shutters down by eight; they had even carted off Babul, the eighteen-year-old who ran a rival den just across from Nasir bhai's, to the thana. Nasir bhai, being an old resident of the basti, was better connected. Just the other day Angad had been woken up by a cop prodding him in the ribs with a rifle butt. Angad, paralysed by visions of prison, had remained glued to his bench till Nasir bhai ambled over and introduced him to the policeman. All three had ended up sharing the same chillum.

Ilyas emptied out a Cavenders cigarette and made a joint. 'I really must go now,' said Angad, 'I don't think I'll get any autos at this hour.'

'Not to worry, hero. There's one auto guy who comes around eleven-thirty to pick up a wrap. We'll fix you up with him.' Ilyas handed the joint to Angad who lit it on the second match.

Stories flew thick and fast around Angad. Dheeraj threw in an armful of garbage and old newspapers into the dying fire. Bits of paper, cloth and plastic went up in a big ball of smoke. Heera, a former truck driver, had joined the circle. Angad had seen him around on previous occasions. Short and well built, with a pair of gleaming black beads for eyes, Heera was usually dressed in uniform: sky blue shirt, matching trousers and plastic chappals. He now worked as a cabbie, driving taxis between Delhi and Dehra Dun, where he lived. Each time he was in Delhi to pick or drop someone, he made it a point to come to Nasir bhai's parlour. Heera was famous for his rambling monologues. He was a good storyteller and had no problems when it came to finding an audience.

Today, he had walked in looking extremely flustered: 'Delhi girls I tell you—they're faster than my Indica. Was at the ITO intersection when this chicknee pulled up next to my car. I said to her: "My cock, your mouth, love." You know what she did? She winked and drove off, her red lips forming a big gaping O. Ilyas bhai . . . see my hard on? It's been forty minutes since that happened but this frenzy in my crotch refuses to subside. One needs a chillum to deal with this city.'

There were three things Heera loved talking about—the years of early struggle, his tragic marriage and his days as an intercity long haul truck driver.

'Do you know why there are so many coal fires in Dhanbad?' asked Heera, 'Because the English set fire to the mines when they left. They knew that coal was as valuable as gold. And it's the heat from the mines that gives the poor Biharis such dark skins.

'Truck driving has taken me to places I would never have gone to otherwise. I drove these monsters for ten years—not a joke, brother, driving one of these machines. Imagine driving from Delhi to Calcutta, your truck laden with dangerous chemicals. Took fifteen days to go, fifteen to come back. The month was gone before it began.

'I saw a lot, a different landscape each time. Jharkand was

the most dangerous. In those days the separatist movement was on. The guerrillas would set up roadblocks. Once the vehicle had come to a halt, they would shoot arrows at the tyres and deflate them.

'But life is unpredictable. The one lesson I have learnt is that planning gets you nowhere. What's the point wasting time planning things when things are, ultimately, not in your hands?

'I still remember that day as if it was yesterday. I had been married for two years. Beautiful girl—my neighbour from Dehra Dun. It was a love marriage—her brothers created problems initially but things were sorted out soon enough. I was still driving trucks and not getting to meet her as much as I would have liked to.

'Fortunately for us—God was favouring us then—she became pregnant. At the time of her delivery I had to take a consignment all the way to Rajasthan. In Bikaner I decided to go visit the Karni Mata Mandir. The place is crawling with rats. There are thousands and thousands of rodents running on the floor, climbing up the walls. It's extremely dark inside the temple. You don't step in without taking precautions: stuff your trouser bottoms inside knee-length socks, fasten your shirtsleeves to your wrists with handkerchiefs, tie a towel around your shirt collar. Any opening anywhere and the rats will find their way in; very soon you'll have a rat running down your spine. Not a nice feeling. Once inside you have to be careful; don't lift your feet, shuffle. A dead rat means ill luck. The rats are all over you—crawling down your face, up your trouser legs—but the idea is not to get scared. So many people never enter the temple—they come all the way but one look inside and they develop cold feet.

'Anyway, I made it to the shrine inside. Ten minutes seemed like ten thousand. It was raining hard when I emerged from the cave temple. That evening, when I called home, I was told that my wife had died during childbirth.

'That broke me completely. I went crazy. I drank so much that I landed up in hospital. They put sixty-two bottles of glucose in me. Can you believe that—sixty-two motherfucking bottles! The alcohol made me remember the little details, small things about my wife: the first time I met her, the way her eyes lit up when she laughed, the last bonk . . . yes, that too.

'Sometimes I would sit on the same chair, in the same position and cry for hours, days.'

Angad found himself getting depressed by Heera's talk. He felt a sadness welling up inside him. It was a nice numb sadness. Ilyas passed a chillum. He wrapped his fingers around the slender clay pipe and took a few short drags before going for the long pull.

As he was passing the pipe back to Ilyas he caught sight of a figure in a three-piece suit lingering behind a tea shack. The shiny suit looked incongruous in the slum. The man, probably conscious of the attention he was getting, decided to emerge from his hiding place. He stepped out boldly and walked past Ilyas, looking him straight in the eye. Ilyas and Angad fell silent. A couple of minutes later he returned and tried to catch Ilyas' eye again. Ilyas fixed his gaze on the floor and refused to look up.

'Who's he?' asked Angad.

'Comes for me. He's in love but I couldn't be bothered.'

'Do you like that kind of thing?'

'What kind of thing?'

'Do you prefer men to women?'

'Yes, I do. They are more reliable than women. And stronger too.'

'Stronger? Emotionally or physically?'

'Both. You know what? You've got a killer smile. But don't worry,' said Ilyas grabbing Angad's butt, 'we are like brothers.'

Angad smiled his toothpaste ad smile.

Babul, having shut his shop, walked across to where Ilyas and Angad were sitting. Babul owned the shop opposite Nasir bhai's. He got the cooler, younger customers—yuppie lawyers on their way home from work, tall African students who exchanged high fives with him, and long-haired guitarists who played in local bands with names like Bleeding Madras, Buddha's Babies and Karmic Circle. Babul was fond of gadgets; he was always playing with a video game or a Casio pocket diary. No one knew where he got them from and no one asked. Babul was built like a bull—his muscles thick and knotted like strong rope. Sometimes he would play East Bengali folk songs on his tape deck and get all teary-eyed.

Babul sat down, and taking out a calculator began pressing digits on it. He launched into an account of his recent trip to the police thana. They had kept him standing in the murga position for many hours, his head almost touching the ground, his ass raised high in the air, his body a demeaning tangle of arms and legs. 'I felt the blood rush to my head as if a dam had burst,' said Babul. 'Every once in a while a cop would come and kick my behind. I would topple over and fall on the floor. And each time I fell, the havaldars would snigger and call me names.' Babul fell silent for a while, the memory of the humiliation seemed to seal his lips. He went back to the calculator. Then he looked up and said, 'If I ever get the chance I'd like to stick hot rods up their mothers' cunts.' Ilyas and Angad did not say anything.

Meanwhile Heera, his small crowd of listeners undiminished, was still going strong:

'I've met my fair share of Bollywood stars. Real big ones. I've driven so many of them around that I don't remember the names of half of them. Satish Kaushik was one—you know that guy in *Mr India*. I was driving like a maniac—like I always do—and he said: "Take it easy, man, I've got loads of films left in me yet!" Pankaj Kapoor and Supriya Pathak were in the same cab.

'But, you know what? I never even dreamed of driving my own cab. I loved climbing trees. When I was thirteen-fourteen and if it was the season, I would take up work in the orchards, plucking litchis, mangoes. Didn't fetch me much money though. I never earned more than ten rupees a day.

'I come from a poor family. My mother worked as a maid in a middle-class neighbourhood. Sometimes, if I finished my homework early, I would accompany her just to see how the other half lived. I made friends with the children of the sahibs. Occasionally they would invite me to join them in a game of cricket. I looked forward to these invitations, except that I was never allowed to bat. I was always the fielder; every once in a while a generous captain would throw me the ball for an odd over or two. I liked bowling leg spin.

'One day, after a longish game, I came back with the sahib's children to their house. My mother had finished her work and was waiting for me. I was thirsty and asked for some water. As usual I was given a steel tumbler while the sahib's children drank out of glasses. Then Dobby, the sahib's son, asked me if I knew what the English word for "pani" was. I didn't. Then he asked me to spell "pencil". When I couldn't he laughed and called me an idiot. I began to cry. My mother saw the entire incident. She marched in, and grabbing hold of my hand, dragged me out of the room.

'I thought: I am fifteen years old and still don't know how to spell "pencil". What's the point of studying any further? I had a friend who worked as a motor mechanic. We both decided to run away from home. One night we boarded the Mussoorie Express to Delhi. We had no tickets. When the ticket examiner came we hid in the toilet. In the morning we made friends with this man who owned a meat shop in Shahdara, near Radhoo Palace Cinema. I had no idea where Shahdara was. This man hired us very cheap. We didn't mind because we got two meals a day and a place to sleep. It was hard work. We would sweat it out from five in the morning till midnight. I slept on a bench at the back of the shop. On the rare day off we would go to Radhoo and watch a film.

'After a couple of months both of us began to miss home; we missed the valley air. My mate was the first to give up the job and return. He wrote to me saying that my parents had spent hundreds of rupees trying to find me; they'd even had posters printed, with my photo in the middle and "MISSING" written on top. The next day I caught the Mussoorie Express back to Dehra Dun.'

It was around one in the morning. The monologues had ceased to flow with Heera deciding to go have a drink somewhere else. Since Dheeraj had gone off to sleep, Ilyas had taken over the bag of weed and the tin can full of cash.

A dopey ennui had taken hold of Ilyas and Angad. As a way out, Ilyas suggested a bottle of spiced country liquor. A kid was dispatched to Gopal's shack with instructions to get a bottle of Masti. 'Get me the bottle, you understand, not some pouch of dubious poison,' Ilyas shouted after the kid, 'or else I'll beat your dirty little ass.'

Angad tipped the boy a tenner when he returned while Ilyas fetched two cups from the smoking parlour. Alcohol always made Ilyas giggly so Angad was not surprised when, after a few quick ones, Ilyas chuckled, 'I guess you are not going back home?'

'I guess not,' replied Angad. 'I can't see what's so funny about it. Let's have dinner.'

By the time dinner arrived—a blob of already-melting butter, six thick rotis and a bowl of watery dal—both men were very drunk, Ilyas more so than Angad. Ilyas tried picking up the butter with his dirty fingers but it kept sliding out of his grasp. This irritated him no end and he let loose a string of expletives: *'Madar chod makhkhan,'* he grumbled, 'I'll fix you,

you son of a whore.' Angad watched in silent disgust as the crescents of dirt under Ilyas' nails gradually disappeared in the butter. The blob fell on Ilyas' crotch where it finally disintegrated. The butter seeped through his trousers, greasing his frizzy pubes. Desperate to save whatever he could of this precious commodity, Ilyas gently dabbed each roti on his filthy crotch as if applying Dettol-soaked cotton wool to a wound. Preliminaries over, they both rearranged themselves, sitting astride each end of the bench like on a seesaw. 'Khao,' barked Ilyas and dinner was underway.

Later that night, in Ilyas' corner of the slum in jhuggi no. 101, TRN Camp, East of Kailash, it was a tight fit. The room was little more than a tiny cubicle with walls of straw and a tarpaulin sheet for a roof. Four small aluminium trunks were arranged symmetrically—one against each of the four walls. In the centre someone had spread out a black velvet bedspread. Two blankets, neatly folded, lay on one of the trunks. The velvet sheet was clearly a loan from Nasir bhai, a little gesture to relieve the poverty of the slum, an attempt to make things more palatable for an unusual guest.

Dheeraj was already asleep next to the trunk on the opposite wall; Ilyas took the space in the middle; Angad settled down next to him. The light was turned out.

Five minutes later there was a terrific commotion behind the trunk next to which Angad was lying. He sat up scared: 'What the fuck was that?'

'Rat. Big fat rat with love handles,' giggled Ilyas, the food having done nothing to temper the Masti in his head. 'Let's swap places. You take the middle if you feel safer here.'

Angad lay on his back waiting for sleep to arrive. There was hardly any place to toss and turn.

Ilyas and Dheeraj snored away steadily like two night trains making up for lost time. Angad was wide awake. There was a pigsty close by. He could hear the pigs grunt and urinate. Once in a while he would hear the sounds of lovemaking—the walls were extremely thin and every kiss, every sigh, every moan came through as clear as a bell. Occasionally, a baby would set up a loud wail and then you could hear the harried mother, half asleep herself, making cooing sounds, talking gibberish, chanting *'so ja re'* like a mantra. Once, a boy sat up screaming, probably a nightmare. Angad heard the irritated jangling of his mother's glass bangles.

Angad consulted his watch. It was around two in the morning. Feeling restless, and unable to sleep, he decided to step out for some fresh air and a smoke. He picked himself up carefully so as not to wake his slumbering neighbours, their bodies as inert as stone pillars.

He searched for his bag which had his pouch of Wills and a book of Capstan papers. Just as he was about to give up he saw the bag lying behind Ilyas' head, and, as he bent to pick it up, he spotted the half-full bottle of Masti lying on the floor. Angad thought for a second, then picked up the bottle—it would be cold outside. He would take a few swigs to keep himself warm, smoke a cigarette and come back.

In the narrow, open corridor outside the cold hit him like a clenched fist. He was glad he had brought the bottle along. At the end of the corridor, instead of turning left towards the smoking parlour, Angad turned right. He went past Mullaji's chicken coop, past the bundles of waste paper stacked up neatly, until he reached a refuse heap. Next to it was a wooden stool. The smell was not as bad as he had expected; on the contrary it was rather sweet, organic, uplifting. He sat down and opened the bottle of liquor.

The cold penetrated his pullover, then his skin; it got into his bones and swirled around in his marrow. In the silver-grey of the moonlight, the basti looked pretty, even picture postcard-like. Two abandoned balloons and scraps of ripped lottery tickets danced about in the wind that was still blowing strong. On the highway that ran parallel to the slum, intercity trucks hurtled down on autopilot, their booze-addled drivers half asleep at the wheel.

Angad drank from the bottle and smoked cigarettes. When he grew tired of the cigarettes, he cleaned out some weed in his palm and smoked a couple of joints. He drank some more. At times he felt that the restlessness that had kept him awake had gone and he should go back to bed. At other moments he felt that a different kind of restlessness had taken hold of him and he would never be able to sleep again. He shuddered at the thought of staying awake for the rest of his life.

Then he found the letters. They were right there in his bag, in the side pocket. The letter Arundhati had written to him soon after they split up; printouts of the last emails, the very last. Angad found himself shaking. The letters were not supposed to be there. Letters meant rotten memories, memories he tried everyday to block: the nasty sentences, the elementary hurt, the horrible sound of something real disintegrating, the bloody sight of love being chopped up on the railway tracks, the foul smell of failure and self-pity.

He knew he should stop drinking now. He knew this wasn't the right time to start re-reading the classics. He knew he should take a couple of Valiums and take his rightful snoring place between Ilyas and Dheeraj in jhuggi no. 101.

But he was seized by a mad desire to read the letters. He felt helpless. There were three printouts and he wanted to read all of them, once again, from beginning to end. He carefully screwed the cap back on the bottle of Masti, put it in the bag with the letters and began to walk.

The highway was as bright as day. The golden light of sodium vapour lamps made the entire stretch look like a stage set. Even though there were no trucks around at the moment, the rumbling of their wheels could be heard in the distance, like the steady roar of an ocean. People were asleep on the pavement, curled up inside their cycle rickshaws. A bearded man, with not a stitch of clothing on his body, stuck his neck out of a rusting Ambassador with flat tyres and made faces at Angad as he walked past. The fog had begun to wrap everything in its cotton wool whiteness. Rectangular pieces of foil tossed about in the wind, the remnants of someone's dragon chase. Angad walked like a man on a mission.

He must have walked for a quarter of an hour before he felt his legs tiring. He saw a green Bajaj Chetak parked on the roadside and decided to rest for a while. He sat astride the driver's seat and closed his eyes, waiting for his breath to catch up. His hands fumbled inside the bag trying to find the letters. He arranged the printouts in the order in which he had received them. His mouth was dry. He had a sip of Masti. He began to read.

The first letter—a proper one on paper—after she walked out on him. Then, the emails that came later, with details of her new boyfriend:

Dear Bebe,

I am very happy. The boy is called Javed Khan and he is a practising Muslim. He is six foot tall, an ex footballer. He is balding and has a big nose. He is a serious techno freak; Dave Clark is a name I hear often. He's also into garage and house etc. He prays all the time and will not marry me becoz it is against his religion to marry a Hindu. It seems his chances of going to paradise reduce . . . hmmm. Well, one meets all types.

But I am happy. He is very caring and my sense of numbness seems to be ebbing away. He makes me feel like I should care for myself. I don't think I give him much but he seems happy to take care of me and tries to solve my problems in whatever way he can. I guess sometimes god sends people just to help you out in times of stress and then they go away.

He bought me my own website for my birthday which is the nicest thing I can think of . . . so now there is an arundhatibannerji.com on the net . . . still under construction as I have to upload my portfolio. I felt very touched. I've been having very painful migraines this past month and he has given me this rare herb that seems to be working wonders.

He is a genuinely nice person. I don't want anything else at this moment.

I'm sorry . . . this must hurt to read but this is my reality.

Every once in a while he goes off to Holland on business. The days he is away I miss the companionship a lot. I read books, go to the gym, freelance. I do miss you but I am changing . . . I HAVE changed. I'm quieter, more introspective, I want different things from life, I want a sense of security and stability, I want simplicity . . . and Javed is fulfilling these needs . . . anyway work beckons.

Ciao,

Arundhati

Hi Bebe,

Have been getting your messages since last night. It would be great if you sent them to me from ICQ coz then I can immediately reply from my mobile. ICQ allows that. My ICQ number is 165053476. Sandy's coming?? He'll come to Calcutta for sure, right? Yipee!

My birthday was surprisingly quite nice . . . I woke up gloomy and wanted to forget that I have just three years before I hit thirty. Had a good cry and listened to Smashing Pumpkins. But I was not allowed to forget it at all.

Javed sent me flowers and planned a surprise cake-and-candle affair in the evening. I wasn't expecting that at all so it was rather nice.

What are you doing today?

Ciao,

A.

Then, the email that came in reply to Angad's pleas for a reunion:

I've told you again and again I have a new life here. I have left everything from last year behind. Things change and keep changing.

In the last two months I have met someone who has helped me regain my will to live and I have come to depend on him enormously.

I have learnt a great deal about myself and my needs. The more I understand and face up to the kind of person I am the more I realize that what we had is over. We cannot and will not be able to regain what we had; the consequences of that can only be as devastating as they were last year. I cannot afford to take another risk.

My youth is tied up with yours; it always will be. Nothing can touch that. As adults we have become two separate people who cannot fulfil each other's needs.

I guess something has changed in you to want decisions like this now but please let this be very clear—nothing has changed for me. I am secure in my world in Calcutta . . . my job, my friends, and I do not want it to change.

I once dreamed of a family that you and I would create. Of a small house, of aspirations realized in love and in work, of peace in each other's arms. But life is a bitter pill to swallow and sometimes things do not work out the way we would like them to.

This dream of mine is broken, Angad, and I do not have the faith to begin it again.

Angad read until the lines went all watery and disappeared from the page. He could read no more. The lights were going out in his head. When the booze finished he threw the bottle into the middle of the road and watched it smash. The noise brought the dogs out. They growled at him; he growled back. One mangy, brown-and-white specimen decided to follow him. Angad chucked the letters on the road and watched them being dragged along in a truck's slipstream.

He was very cold by now. He had forgotten to bring his jacket and cap. The fog formed a thick curtain. Angad could hardly see. He was mumbling to himself. Strange, incoherent thoughts kept popping into his head and out of his mouth: 'Baby, do you remember,' he muttered, 'when your father threw you on a gas stove. You had a black eye, burn marks on your forearm . . . I kissed you there . . . chutiya Sai Baba . . . how could you? You didn't need to . . . she's into Sai Bai—that Slash look alike . . . no, no the other one, the one with the bandana . . . that's right, the Axl Rose look alike . . . let's do a nose rub, boo . . . we could have . . . why did you?' By now Angad had left the main road and turned into a lane. His steps stubbornly refused to trace a straight line.

His head was a spinning top, a mad jumble of broken bangles—a kaleidoscope gone awry. And no amount of turning was going to produce the neat geometrical figures that used to fall into place so effortlessly in the past.

He heard footsteps behind him. He wasn't sure. His brainpan concealed all kinds of voices and sounds. Then he stopped and turned around. There seemed to be two people standing in front of him. 'Hello,' said Angad, 'we're all in it together, mate. It happens to you, it happens to me. My father's a very nice guy, you know. You should meet him sometime.' Then, sensing that something was wrong, Angad said, 'Website. You guys want a website? No problem. I'll give you as many as you want. Flowers too. All the way from Holland. But whatever you do please don't go to the train station. You hear me? Never go to the train station.'

The two boys, both around nineteen, went for him. They punched him in the stomach, then the mouth. As he doubled over they pushed him to the ground from behind. Angad's head hit the side of the pavement. The boys took his wristwatch and emptied out his wallet. They searched the bag but finding nothing inside left it behind.

At around four in the morning, a Delhi Police Gypsy drew up next to where Angad lay face down on the pavement. Two cops got out. One of them began to kick Angad, but, to be fair, he only kicked at the shins and the ankles—he was being kind. The other picked up Angad's bag and, without bothering to check inside, said, 'Chalo, chalo, let's go. It's too cold here.'

When Angad opened his eyes, he felt a hot tongue on his forehead, he tasted blood on his own tongue. There were dogs all around him, drawn, no doubt, by the sight of his crumpled body, intrigued by the smell of his blood. When he tried to pick himself up they backed away snarling.

Back in Okhla Basti, it was seven in the morning. People were spitting, shitting, having sweet, milky tea, getting ready for a new day. Ilyas was smoking his first chillum. '*Jai, jai, Shiv Shankar, na kaanta lage na kankar,*' he chanted, before taking the mother of all pulls. A sadhu—Tiger Baba—sat next to him, sharing the chillum and coughing his tubercular cough. The morning lot had begun to arrive for their fix. Opposite Nasir bhai's parlour, the old man who bred racing pigeons pottered about outside his shack, cleaning his teeth with a neem twig. At night he covered the cages with gunnysack in order to keep the pigeons warm. He walked up and down, neem twig in mouth, single-handedly removing the sacks. The pigeons hopped about randomly, setting up a huge racket as soon as they felt the first rays of the sun on their backs. The old man's wife stood framed in the kitchen window. A pressure cooker blew steam in her face.

By now Dheeraj had joined Ilyas and Tiger Baba. They watched the old man at work with his pigeons. Soon he would open the doors to the cages and the birds would be all over him. 'Where's Angad?' asked Dheeraj, 'I woke up at six and he wasn't there.' 'Must have gone home at some point,' said Ilyas. 'Must have taken a cab. One night in the slum probably proved too much for babyface. Left behind his jacket and cap though.'

The Teacher's Daughter

On 2 November 1984, Keshav Tripathi woke up with a terrible sinus headache. He lay in bed waiting for the pain to subside. When it didn't, he called out to his wife and asked for a glass of hot water. She was in the balcony at the back of the flat, putting clothes out to dry. Not getting a reply, Tripathi roared in irritation, 'Sudha, can you get me a glass of hot water. My head's hurting again.' Sudha rushed into the room a couple of minutes later and in a weary voice asked her husband why he was raising a racket this early in the morning. 'My sinus,' said Tripathi, pointing to his forehead. 'It's acting up again. Can you get me a glass of hot water ... *please*?' Sudha turned around without replying and walked in the direction of the kitchen, muttering something.

Tripathi and Sudha had been married for twenty-five years now but her barbs still retained the power to incense him. He would get so worked up, he would begin muttering to himself. What really got his goat was the lack of clarity: why was she upset with him? What had he done? What was she saying?

Tripathi lay in bed, sipping the hot water his wife had

brought for him. 'It's too hot,' he complained. 'If you grumbled less, and kept your ears open and your mind free of clutter, you would get things right more often.' Sudha wasn't in the mood for an argument this morning. There was too much work around the house. Still, she couldn't resist, 'If you smoked less, you wouldn't have the problem in the first place. I am not saying give up, but you can try and cut down at least. Now, did I just say that for the millionth time?' Not wanting to prolong the discussion, she quickly changed the subject, 'Jyoti has an exam. You have invigilation. If you don't get up now you'll never make it in time and the poor girl will lose a year.'

Tripathi hauled himself out of bed with great effort. He shuffled towards the lone toilet in the house in his round-necked, short-sleeved vest and chequered boxers, only to find it occupied. 'Hurry up, Jyoti,' he said in a robotic voice. 'We're getting late.'

Jyoti studied at the same provincial university her father taught at. Her parents saw her as a quiet girl with no clear-cut interests. Her elder sister Aarti was the star of the family—head girl in school, general secretary of the students' union in medical college, now married to a fellow doctor. 'Aarti is doing so well in Nagpur,' the mother would brag to the neighbours, 'but Jyoti's such a simple girl. We'll marry her off by the time she finishes her degree. If you have someone in mind, then do let us know.'

Jyoti joined the BA course following her parents' wishes. Her heart wasn't in it though. Her father had been teaching the same English course for the last thirty years but was as clueless as her about Byron, Shelley and Keats. Still, they both soldiered on.

Today was the day of the re-examination. When Jyoti sat for her prose paper earlier in the year, there had been complaints of irregularities. A section of the students insisted that the paper had been leaked before the examination actually took place. They organized a protest outside the vice chancellor's office and chanted slogans. The VC, wanting to avoid an unpleasant scene, ordered a fresh examination scheduled for the next term.

Tripathi and his daughter set out from home at the stroke of eight. She wore a blue salwar kameez, her long thick hair was held in place by two shiny black pins. She sat sideways on her father's scooter, her cracked heels planted firmly on the aluminium footrest.

When Jyoti was five years old, she used to stand in front, her tiny palms gripping the handle. As she grew older and taller, she began obstructing her father's line of sight. He would slide back a bit, thus freeing a tiny amount of space on which Jyoti would perch precariously. Then, one day, the front of the scooter became too cramped to contain both father and daughter. Jyoti found herself banished to the middle of the vehicle. Right through middle school she sat in that position, a tender slice of ham sandwiched between two crusty slices of bread.

By the time she entered 12th standard, the LML Vespa could only fit two. If the family was calling on friends, Tripathi would put wife and daughter in a cycle rickshaw and follow on his scooter.

~~

Tripathi was a short, squat man. He liked wearing dull colours. His preferred fabric was terry cotton because it was easy to wash and required no ironing. He liked wearing his shirts outside his trousers. He found shoes constricting, generally preferring to move about in Sandtek flip-flops.

During the years Jyoti sat between her parents on the Vespa, Tripathi noticed something unusual. Jyoti seemed to add inches to her height almost everyday.

At the beginning of one year, he felt her nose bumping halfway up his spine. By the end of that year, the nose had reached up to his shoulders, another few months and she was literally breathing down his neck. By the time she finished school she had shot past his scratched and faded yellow helmet—a good head taller than him. Nowadays, on certain winter evenings, coming back with her father on the scooter after doing some shopping, Jyoti would feel the cold wind on her face and wish for the days of her childhood to return. Back then, she was the warmest, happiest child on any road, anywhere in the world. Her wobbly back propped up by her mother's comfortable arm, her face squashed sideways on her father's back, her hands clasped around his substantial paunch, Jyoti would feel so safe and contented that she would sometimes even fall asleep. She would open her eyes ever so slightly at a noisy traffic intersection, then slip back into her reverie.

~~

Tripathi and Jyoti barely made it in time for her examination. Tripathi walked down the corridor towards the staffroom. The plaster had come off in various places giving the place the look of an unfinished jigsaw puzzle, half the pieces having fallen off at some point. Most of the furniture in the classrooms was broken. Disgruntled men had been letting off steam in these high-ceilinged rooms for decades. The windowpanes were all shattered; jagged pieces of glass remained stuck in the frames like stubborn natives broken and dispossessed by foreign invaders, yet refusing to leave.

Tripathi walked into the staffroom and lowered himself into a chair whose springs had packed up long since. The faulty springs meant he had to sit at a strange angle. He had been in this place for almost thirty years now—the slant didn't even register. He unfolded the day's *Northern India Patrika*. It was still carrying news of Indira Gandhi's assassination. Tripathi took little interest in politics. The news of the murder had not affected him personally like it had his wife who, like her mother, always voted Congress.

He ran his eyes over the television listings and cursed the government. Tripathi was a TV addict. These days, because of the prime minister's assassination, Doordarshan was in mourning mode. Tripathi wanted *Chitrahaar* and *Hum Log*. What he got instead was *Shraddhanjali*, *Century of Surgeons*, *The Living Planet*, Films Division documentaries. Sometimes a mischievous programming editor slipped in a Russian circus, the recording of a P.C. Sorcar magic show. The cheerful Bengali pranced around the stage guillotining unsuspecting victims, before disappearing into a tiny tin trunk the size of a school satchel. Every ten minutes, he picked up an ornate jug placed at the corner of the stage and poured water out of it.

The thing to marvel at was the apparently bottomless nature of the vessel—the 'Water of India' never stopped flowing. This particular trick involving Miracle Jug and Eternal River never failed to raise Tripathi's ire. Once, he had even taken off his chappal and thrown it at the television screen. This upset Mrs Tripathi no end. She called up her father and complained to him about the kind of man he had chosen for her to spend the rest of her life with.

Tripathi sat on a chair on the stage and looked down at the rows of students hunched over their desks, scribbling. He was head invigilator. There were two other invigilators in the hall—young chemistry lecturers who had just joined and were on probation. Tripathi maintained his distance from them.

His sinuses had started to act up again. Tripathi gestured to the peon to fetch him a glass of hot water. He then fished out a small bottle of Vicks Vaporub from the front pocket of his shirt and, scooping out a small quantity with his index finger, proceeded to rub it into the vertical furrows that lay between his leafy eyebrows.

Occasionally, he would spot someone peeking into someone else's answer script, a student whispering a query to a fellow student. Tripathi's policy in these instances was to stare and ignore. The rest he left to the chemistry lecturers. After all, he was head invigilator. It would be beneath his dignity to be seen walking amongst the proletarian rows.

An hour before the examination was supposed to end Tripathi received a note from the controller of examinations, R.P. Yadav, asking to see him before he left for the day. Yadav and Tripathi were not the best of friends. They never acknowledged each other's presence unless it was absolutely unavoidable.

The door to Yadav's room was open. He sat behind an oval table, his elbows resting on the green felt, his flunkies ranged around the table's edges like fielders on the boundary line. 'Come, come, Tripathiji,' said Yadav, pointing to an empty chair. He turned his swivel chair around so that it faced the open windows of his office and fixed his gaze quite deliberately on a neem tree in the grounds outside. The flunkies had fallen silent.

Yadav pulled out a rolled-up sheet of paper from a drawer in his desk. He removed the rubber band and handed it to Tripathi. It was his daughter's answer script. A diagonal red line bisected the front page into two symmetric triangles. A small note scribbled on the bottom left corner of the page said: 'Caught using unfair means'.

Tripathi walked slowly towards the scooter stand. His daughter was supposed to meet him there but was nowhere to be seen. Tripathi handed the attendant his parking token, slipped on his helmet and headed off in the direction of Civil Lines. He was furious with Yadav. That low caste bastard targeting his daughter like this. He remembered Yadav showing him the crib sheets that had been recovered from Jyoti. 'This is the cheating material which I am going to attach to this script as evidence. The rest is up to the committee,' Yadav had said, gesticulating in the direction of the ceiling.

On reaching Civil Lines the first thing Tripathi did was to stop at his bank. He filled in a pink slip and queued up at window number 2. The cashier looked up for a second when Tripathi handed him the slip—the amount was far more than Tripathi usually withdrew.

Tripathi stood to the side of the window and counted the amount. He did not arrange the money in his wallet but stuffed it in the front pockets of his trousers. Leaving the scooter in the bank's parking lot, he headed off towards El Chico, the most expensive restaurant in town. In his youth he would often come here on winter evenings for a cup of coffee. Back in the 'seventies, it had been the first in town to acquire an espresso machine.

Tripathi spent a long time reading the three menus—Chinese, Continental and Mughlai. The waiter approached him for the order but he waved him away impatiently. He wasn't ready yet. He still had to make up his mind. When he had finally decided he piled up the menus neatly, one on top of the other. He raised his left hand in the air like an eager schoolboy desperate to answer a question.

Tripathi ordered so many dishes that the waiter wanted to know if someone else was supposed to join him; if the table required more plates, cutlery, napkins. The food arrived in waves: lung fung soup, chicken Manchurian, vegetable fried rice, sweet and sour vegetable, crispy fried noodles and American chopsuey, a bewildered fried egg occupying the centre of the bowl. Tripathi rubbed his hands together, spread a napkin on his lap, lowered his lips to bowl level, and gently blew into the soup.

He stayed in El Chico for an hour and a half. He ate very little and left most of the food untouched. When he asked for the bill the waiter offered to pack the food but Tripathi refused. He picked up his helmet and walked out into the afternoon sunshine, but not before he had left a generous tip, his fattest ever.

Still not in a mood to go home, he decided to wander around Civil Lines for a while. He walked into shops at random. He walked into Gangotri and made the young salesgirl pull out piles of bed sheets from the shelf behind her. He did not buy any.

He walked into B.N. Rama Stores and wandered around the toys section. A remote-controlled car with a red revolving light caught his fancy. He played with it for a while, mesmerized. His lips opened and shut in constant movement but no word or sound escaped them. Every few seconds, his left hand would fly up in the air emphasizing a point in a private argument.

Back on the pavement outside, he was seized by a violent craving for ice cream. He turned left from B.N. Rama's and walked in a straight line till he reached HotBite, the town's only fast-food joint and ice cream parlour. The place was full of young people, mostly teenaged boys, talking loudly and excitedly. Christmas decorations were already in place. Balloons floated listlessly in the air-conditioned air, fairy lights blinked on and off ceaselessly, oversized stars dangled from the ceiling like cheerful corpses.

A group of boys instinctively fell silent when they saw Tripathi walk in. They resumed their animated discussion when they saw him take a table far removed from theirs.

Tripathi sat with his back to everybody. He had walked in for an ice cream but once inside felt like ordering a large quantity of food and gobbling it up in one go.

He walked back to the counter and ordered food worth several hundred rupees. When his turn came, it took him three trips to get the food to his table. He arranged the trays carefully as if following a pre-conceived plan.

An hour went by and Tripathi didn't even realize it. The food remained untouched. Had he ordered all of this? The 29.5 cm paneer tikka 'n' green chilli pizza, the spicy chicken fillet burger, the capsicum onion mushroom footlong, the chicken kathi roll, the pint glass full of hot chocolate fudge. He picked up the fork and began playing with the jalapeño peppers on his pizza.

He was worried for Jyoti. Did she really have to do this? She had failed the paper last year. The news of the leaked paper and the ordering of the re-examination had come as a godsend. Now, it was all over. Yadav was his enemy and he would make sure things didn't get any easier.

How on earth was he supposed to marry her off now? Her oily skin was not going to transform overnight, was it? The pimples on the face were not going to vanish just like that, were they? The frizzy hair, well, she got that from her mother. And the complexion, dark as night . . . now where did that come from? Who would want to marry her? Ugly, 12th pass, Hindi medium. With a BA degree there was a chance that an educated family might accept her. A widower with baggage

was the only hope now. Even he wasn't going to come easy.
Tripathi groaned loudly, audibly, at the thought of the huge
dowry he would have to raise in order to clinch a deal with
this notional widower.

The minutes ticked by in the crowded restaurant. Tripathi's
mind felt numb. He was unable to think any thoughts. His
hearing, on the other hand, had become very acute, as if his
entire being had transformed itself into a highly sensitive
microphone. He could hear the cooks squabbling in the kitchen,
the man at the counter whispering orders into a mike, a
customer at the next table complaining about the cheese, a
group of boys—their voices vaguely familiar—talking about
condoms. The last conversation held his attention.

One of the boys had gone into the grocer's store next door
and asked for a packet of Kamasutra condoms, 'Bhainchod, sun
na. I asked him for KS condoms, OK? This fucker gets a ladder,
squirrels up to the top shelf, comes down clutching a jar of
something. I'm like, "What's this, dude?" He replies, "Kayam
churan, sir, isn't that what you asked for?"' The entire group
erupted with laughter at the punch line. They stomped their
shoes on the floor and banged their fists on the table. They
roared loudly, inadvertently shooting tiny globules of spit into
the air.

Tripathi felt his temper rise, the brief period of calm
punctured by the boys' conversation, the bullshit excitement.
He picked up his helmet and turned around. He located the
boys and walked, almost strode, towards them. When they
saw him they fell silent. They stood up respectfully and said,

'Good morning, sir,' in unison. Some of the customers turned around to see what was going on.

Tripathi was taken aback for a second or two. He recognized some of the boys from his third-year class. They must know about his daughter. 'Look at yourselves,' he boomed. 'Take a good look in the mirror, each one of you. Spoilt brats, all. Condoms, sex, yes, it's all a bloody joke, life is a bloody joke. Sit in Civil Lines and grind your family name to pulp. Shame on you.'

The boys dropped their heads in mock shame and apologized. Two of them, unable to suppress their laughter, excused themselves and moved away in the direction of the water cooler. Did one of them hiss something about Jyoti? Tripathi couldn't tell.

He stormed out of the restaurant and was immediately surrounded by street children. They sniggered and scattered when he hit out at them with his battered helmet. He went as fast as his scooter could take, weaving in and out of the traffic in a way he hadn't done since he got married. He was desperate to meet Jyoti. After all, she was his daughter; he should be there for her. Of course, he loved her. Still, she had no business behaving like this. They needed to talk. They would work something out.

He was almost halfway home when he realized he wasn't carrying his license with him. To get to his house he had to drive past a traffic police checkpoint. Every evening, from five till about nine, the policemen flagged down two-wheelers and checked for licenses. Tripathi looked inside his wallet. Hopefully he had enough to bribe them. The wallet was empty apart from a five-rupee note. He had spent the rest in El Chico and HotBite.

Touch and Go

Ambuj Goel sat in his office staring out of the lone window in the room. The rain fell in torrents, like it had for the last few days. It was a deadening rain, the kind which not only makes normal life impossible but also shutters the mind.

Goel felt tired which was odd because he hadn't been working too hard. A civil servant by profession, he had recently been transferred to Dehra Dun. The office was still waiting for the bulk of the files to be shifted from Lucknow, the previous headquarters. There was a lot of waiting to do and, meanwhile, a lot of rain.

Goel led a quiet bachelor's existence. Although he was new to the town he had already made his acquaintance with a few locals, one of them, Ed Faleiro, a novelist whose books he greatly admired. Faleiro was much younger than him. He lived in a crumbling, colonial house, not too far from the secretariat where Goel worked. Goel often drove down to his place after office hours. He never stayed for long, usually leaving after a cup of tea. The novelist, on his part, didn't mind Goel's visits. He led an isolated and solitary life. He welcomed the half-hour interruptions, three or four times a week.

On the occasional clear day, when it wasn't raining, they would sit on the terrace, sipping lemon tea, not saying very much. Goel would have loved to talk about Faleiro's novels but he wasn't encouraged in this.

At thirty-six, Faleiro had written four novels and exuded the air of someone who had been writing for decades. He was not excitable in the least, spoke very little and seldom moved out of the house. At around half six in the evening, he'd walk down to the baker at the corner of the street and buy a loaf of wholemeal bread. On the way back, he might pick up a pack of cigarettes or a dozen eggs from the grocer's. Faleiro was a quiet, routine-bound man who hated casual banter. The baker and the grocer had learnt to keep their mouths shut and refrained from making unnecessary conversation about the weather and inflation.

Faleiro never spoke about his personal life. Sometimes, when Goel went to his place, he'd find a young woman who'd come visiting from Delhi or Bombay or even abroad. In front of Goel, Faleiro and his lady friends always maintained a formal distance. It was impossible for him to tell if they were lovers, ex-lovers or friends. Goel knew it was none of his business, and that he shouldn't be interested in people's private affairs. Still, no matter how hard he tried, he couldn't help wondering.

Lying alone in bed at night, Goel often thought about the life he was leading: a bachelor posted in small towns, working like a dog, filling his day with files. He was an honest officer. Every now and then his honesty had got him into trouble but he never let it get to him. He liked a bit of push and pull. His uprightness didn't stem from idealism but habit and convenience. Rules were meant to be followed. Things were simpler that way.

The continuously falling rain, the darkened mornings and afternoons, the rain worms crawling out of cracks in the old floor tiles, the snails torturously making their way across the verandah of his house—all these things had conspired to fill Goel with strange desires.

That evening, circling his desk in office, he experienced tremendous boredom. He also felt curiously inspired. He was supposed to meet Faleiro at 5.30. Since it was raining they would have to sit inside. Goel preferred sitting inside. He liked the way the muted rays from the standard lamp lit up Faleiro's fine and delicate features. Goel would then observe him, slyly and intensely, like a smitten child admiring his football hero.

He left his office at the stroke of five. The car had problems starting. Goel regretted having dismissed the driver. Finally, the engine responded and Goel reversed blindly on to the main road. The gears were heavy and unresponsive. He realized he was driving with his handbrake on and immediately released it.

Faleiro had just finished a chapter and seemed in good spirits. They sat in a room on the first floor of the house. The red-coloured floor had green and black borders running along the sides. Rafters held up the sagging ceiling. There was no electricity, so they sipped their tea in the murky light, their conviviality undimmed by the power cut.

Faleiro was unusually talkative today. He spoke about how good it felt when pieces in the plot jigsaw fell into place, when characters began speaking in their own voices. He spoke of it as a rare occurrence, as unusual as the sighting of an elusive beast. It happened every once in a while, said Faleiro, and it had happened today.

Goel liked it when Faleiro spoke excitedly and fluently. He knew his job was to listen and pretend to understand, even when he didn't understand very much.

Faleiro filled an aluminium kettle with water for more tea. It was getting on to six. The rain continued to fall, stopping abruptly for a few deceiving minutes, then resuming with its earlier intensity. Faleiro, despite his high spirits, couldn't resist a complaint. 'I wish the power supply wasn't so erratic. It would make this relentless rain a little more tolerable,' he said, switching the gas off.

'Do you think it's a good idea to go out?' Goel asked tentatively, ready for a rejection. He sounded like a son asking his father for an outing, quietly expecting a 'no' because Daddy was busy today and had no time to spare.

'Go where?' asked Faleiro, sounding a little bewildered at the thought of the outside world. 'Go where in this weather?'

'Well,' said Goel, almost withdrawing his proposition, feeling embarrassed at having made such a preposterous suggestion in the first place, 'I thought since we are trapped here in complete darkness, and since you have finished a chapter ... maybe ... I don't know ... I thought we could escape this rain and darkness for once and go someplace else, do something silly.'

'Like what?' asked Faleiro, dipping a Taj Mahal teabag in hot water. Goel shone light from a steel torch while Faleiro squeezed lemon into the cups: 'Let's go and watch a really silly Bollywood film.'

To Goel's relief, Faleiro seemed to like the idea. 'Excellent, let's do it,' he said, as if he had been waiting for Goel to make this suggestion, 'I haven't been to one in ages.'

Prabhat was one of the oldest cinema halls in town. It had stained glass windows depicting scenes from popular Bollywood films: Shah Rukh and Madhuri and Karisma in *Dil To Pagal Hai*, Amitabh gritting his teeth in *Zanjeer*. Goel bought popcorn and coffee. The hall was more or less empty. The plot of the film involved a female pop star and a psychopathic stalker. The pop star theme meant plenty of songs. In the posters, the film had been advertised as a musical thriller.

The cushioning in the seats was loose and uneven, so you could end up with one buttock on a higher plane than the other. The once-flexible backrests had been fixed into rigidity by years of use and abuse. When Faleiro moved his feet, they hit something under the chair. There was a clattering sound and he felt his sandals getting wet and sticky. A bottle of Fanta rolled out, the liquid still oozing from its narrow mouth. He stood up muttering and excused himself to go to the washroom. When he returned, Goel suggested they move further down the row. Faleiro agreed.

On the big screen, Urmila Matondkar danced with spectacular primal energy. She jerked and shuddered, winked and smiled, then pouted at rows and rows of empty seats. Goel checked his luminous dial for the time. They were halfway through the film. The first part had been a series of extravagant disco songs. Another fifteen minutes remained to the interval.

Goel was sitting to the left of Faleiro. Big ceiling fans jutted at right angles from the wall, tirelessly circulating the clammy air. Goel was a big man and felt constricted in the cinema hall seat. He decided to take a break and go to the washroom. He peed and washed his hands in tap water, avoiding the sliver of green soap lying on the side of the basin. The humidity in the hall had made him sticky. He splashed water on his face. He pulled out an oversized handkerchief from his pocket and dabbed his cheeks and forehead with it. He looked at himself in the mirror. His face had a natural grimace which women often found sexy. Although in his early fifties, he had the hair of a young man—luxuriant, unruly and jet-black in colour.

The interval was only five minutes away when Goel returned to his seat. He sat down, folded his palms on his lap and leaned back as far as the seat could go. Casually, he put out his right hand and placed it on Faleiro's left thigh. He didn't press down or anything but let it rest lightly. Faleiro didn't respond. His body didn't tighten from revulsion or fear. He didn't ask Goel to remove it. He sat there, looking straight at the screen and laughed loudly at a joke in the film. Goel, feeling bolder, pressed down a little. Not encountering any resistance even now, he pressed down further. Within seconds, he had his fingers wrapped around Faleiro's slender thigh.

The lights came on. He turned towards Faleiro, searching for a clue. Did he approve? Did he disapprove? Was he disgusted? Faleiro said he needed to stand up, stretch his legs. Goel removed his palm. 'I'm going out into the lobby. Can I get you something, a coffee, a Coke?' Goel declined politely. He said he didn't feel like anything at the moment.

Goel kept his hands to himself for the remainder of the film. He felt annoyed with himself, annoyed with Faleiro, annoyed with the rain.

After the film, Goel suggested they have dinner. Faleiro, though not averse to the idea, explained he couldn't eat until he'd had a drink or two. 'We can have a drink at my place,' said Goel, 'it's not too far from here. We can go to Yeti afterwards for dinner.' Faleiro seemed to like the idea. He had never been to Goel's house, never expressed a desire to visit. Goel was happy that he was coming today, but also a little nervous.

The front room of the house doubled as an office. Plastic chairs lined the wall. A Formica table occupied the centre of the room. Goel led Faleiro inside, to his bedroom. He wondered what Faleiro was thinking. He probably found this place awful.

The bedroom wasn't sarkari at all. Novels and volumes of poetry lined a tall, elegant bookcase. A square-shaped glass almirah held Goel's Hindustani classical collection. Goel took out a bottle of Black Label from a small bedside cabinet and poured two drinks.

Faleiro couldn't stop talking about the film. He pointed

out logical loopholes in the plot, shook his head at the absurdities. Goel was happy to listen to him but couldn't help feeling that Faleiro was trying to avoid something. He was filling the air with rapid-fire analysis in order to avoid silence.

After the first drink, the conversation seemed to have run its course. Faleiro suggested they have another one before dinner. Goel refilled the glasses. He was going to do whatever Faleiro wanted him to.

He was about to hand Faleiro his glass when the power went off. Goel's servant materialized from the kitchen, holding a lit candle. Changing the subject, Faleiro said he had always been interested in Hindustani classical but it seemed to him the kind of thing which required some help—one couldn't start off just like that, the way one did with rock music.

Goel said he'd be happy to lend his CDs. They could spend some time listening to ragas together. He could point things out to Faleiro. There were good concerts coming up in Delhi in October. Maybe they could go for those.

Faleiro nodded but didn't say anything. He was thinking about something else. Goel wondered if he had said too much.

Dinner was a quiet affair. There were few customers, probably because of the rain. A lady at the adjoining table complained loudly that the Thai green curry was not as good as last time, that standards were slipping. Goel ordered a plate of fish and chips and Faleiro, a club sandwich. They ate in silence. At one point Goel said the fish was very fresh; would Faleiro like to try some? 'Sure,' said Faleiro, extending his fork across the table.

They drove back through wet, empty streets. The rain had slowed to a drizzle. Faleiro asked if he could smoke in the car. 'Smoke as many as you want,' Goel said, rolling down his window, 'I used to smoke till very recently. Then I quit.'

'Really? Was it difficult?'

'Yes and no. My servant used to go every morning to get me a pack of Marlboro Lights. One day, when he was handing me the pack after breakfast, I thought to myself: screw it! I told him to keep the cigarettes. He's a smoker himself. Bas, that was it. I haven't smoked since.'

Faleiro lit a second cigarette. Goel looked at his watch, then turned his head to gaze at the empty roads. Not even eleven, yet not a soul in sight. The shops all shuttered. Very few streetlights. Darkness everywhere. He turned to Faleiro and said, 'You know something? I really admire you at times. How have you managed to live here for so long? I'll die if I don't get a transfer to Delhi soon. This town is such a fucking shithole.'

The Nick of Time

Mayank woke at two in the morning and thought it was closer to two in the afternoon. This happened to him often.

He had been in Oxford for a year. Twelve months down the line he was still struggling to come to terms with the weather. The sky remained overcast for weeks on end, an untiring drizzle fell over scowling gargoyles and the tops of umbrellas, slid off the shoulders of raincoats. A uniform light coloured the day, regardless of the hour.

Mayank's sense of time had lost its centre. Some days seemed to pass by too quickly, just vanish into thin air. A snap of the fingers and they were gone. Others would drag interminably, every second that passed a grim reminder that another one was just round the corner, and then another, and another.

One evening he met an Indian girl in a pub just off St Giles. She had big round eyes, long black hair and a glistening, brown complexion. She was a genuine Indian beauty all right. She had been in Oxford for four years now. She started talking about her PhD thesis almost as soon as they met. Mayank scrunched his eyebrows and pretended to listen. He tried to follow but couldn't. He heard four words repeated again and again: the Mughals, feminism, memoir, Persian. That was all that registered.

These days he lived in a state of almost permanent distraction. People would say things but his mind would wander. His eyes would invariably follow his mind until they were no longer focussed on the person he was sitting with. His forehead remained bunched up in feigned concentration but the eyes would drift. They were not vacant eyes though. They would alight and fix on random objects, innocuous mannerisms. For some reason, his eyes kept returning to the tap of Stella Artois in the middle of the bar. There was nothing strange about this tap. It was a tap like any other tap of draught Stella in hundreds of pubs across Britain. Another object of his disinterested, drifty curiosity was an old man standing at the bar drinking pints of Graduate's bitter. He smoked a cigarette with each pint. Before smoking he would break off the end, maybe half a centimetre or so, and discard it in the ashtray. It was a curious game of give and take, of love and hate, a comfortable cycle of pointless revenge: if each cigarette shortens my life by two minutes, I am going to shorten each cigarette's life by half an inch.

Swati noticed this gap between furrowed brow and wandering gaze. She was no fool. After all, she was doing a PhD at Oxford. She was not going to sit here talking like an idiot to an Indian male who seemed to have eyes for everything but no ears for her. 'How typically Indian,' she thought to herself. She was certainly not going to take this lying down.

'Mayank,' she said quietly, 'what's wrong with you? Are

you okay? I have been speaking to you for the last half an hour. I am quite sure you have not followed a word of what I've just said. Is anything the matter? Am I boring you?'

Mayank felt embarrassed. He apologized profusely. He tried to defend himself. 'Swati, please don't get me wrong. I really appreciate you asking me out for a drink. Otherwise I would have been in the PPE reading room, trying to figure out Kant's transcendental deduction and not getting anywhere. You know things are not easy . . .' Mayank felt the words drying up. He stopped speaking.

'What's not easy?' asked Swati, a little puzzled, 'Kant or . . .'

'Look,' said Mayank haltingly, searching for the right words, 'nothing's easy. One works hard to get here only to find that . . . I don't know . . . one's day to day life might be simpler than back home . . . I miss my girlfriend, Swati, I really do. We split up before I left India but I still miss her. I didn't want to separate. She was the one who kept insisting. She said I didn't know how big the world was, that long-distance things never work. I hate it here without her. I hate the weather. I could sleep all day. And I can't concentrate on my readings. I read the same passage again and again without getting anywhere. I find the people here sullen unless they are drunk. Not like back home where you could knock on anyone's door at any time. I really don't know, I'm sorry I'm rambling.'

'Hey,' said Swati, lightly touching his forearm, 'relax, yaar. You don't need to be so uncomfortable with me. I understand. It happened to me too. Took me almost two years before I got my bearings. And then, just when things looked like settling down, Altaf got a teaching offer from Harvard. It's been tough ever since he left. I miss him. I miss a man's touch.'

Mayank nodded in sympathy and looked into her eyes. They stared back at him warmly, expectantly. 'You know what, Mayank?' began Swati. It was her turn now to let her gaze wander, 'Altaf's an old man. Well, he's middle-aged but sometimes he seems so frigging old to me. I need to be touched by a younger person, someone who will explore me like a foreign country, surprise me, surprise himself. I am tired of Altaf's experienced hands, always touching the right spots at the right time.'

When she finished she returned her gaze to Mayank. The pub had become fairly noisy by now. Some Indian students from Mayank's college walked in; one of them winked at him when he saw him sitting with a girl. But Mayank did not notice. He was too busy looking at Swati. 'I think I know what you mean,' he said shyly.

Mayank lives in a squat new building overlooking a football field. On the afternoon of a soccer match, girls crowd the windows on the first floor. They sit on the ledges, cheering their college on, their shapely legs dangling like dead meat. Mayank doesn't much care for soccer but likes the way the girls sound. On days when he is trying to work on an essay, he lets himself be distracted by these high-pitched foreign voices.

Mayank knows the owner of one of these voices. Her name is Libby. She is Canadian. This Michaelmas they are tutorial partners. It's an uneasy relationship. Deadlines are important for Libby. She always meets them. Mayank works differently. If he does not understand something then deadlines can go fuck themselves. He does not see the point of meeting one just for the sake of it.

Sometimes, he goes to Libby's room to borrow a book on the reading list. She is always eating something. Mayank doesn't care much for food but he still feels bad that she doesn't offer him whatever she is munching or sucking on. Often, when he gets back to his room his mind wanders. Instead of sitting down at his table, he gets even more distracted. He feels slighted—she could have at least offered me a cookie . . . of course, I would have refused . . . imagine this happening in India. God, these people are so selfish. On occasion, he gets so worked up that he cannot concentrate on anything—the Matsui television he bought from Dixon's, the Isaac Bashevis Singer he borrowed from the English faculty library across the road, the prescribed text for the term: Immanuel Kant's *The Critique of Pure Reason*. He paces the room, his legs trying hard to keep pace with his racing mind.

He takes out his smoking bag. It contains blue Rizla papers, a dark green pouch of Golden Virginia and a bright yellow pack of Swan filter tips. He rolls a cigarette for himself and lights it with a small Bic lighter. The smoke alarm goes off as if on cue. Mayank pulls the lone easy chair in the room to a spot just under the fire alarm. He clambers on to it and fans the affected area with a copy of *Hello!* magazine till the tweeting subsides. He is a tall man. When he stands on the chair, his head almost touches the ceiling. Libby's room lies on the other side. Sometimes he wishes that the ceiling was not made of concrete, or that he was blessed with superhuman powers. In that magical scenario he knows exactly what he would do.

He would extend his hand into her room where it would nose around like a periscope, then reach out and pluck the jar of cookies from the shelf, the same cookies Libby had been eating just a couple of hours earlier, cookies that would never be shared with him. The hand would tighten its grip and, when Libby was looking the other way, withdraw to Mayank's room.

Mayank and Swati walked back to his room along the cobbled pavement that ran alongside the chemistry labs. He had his arms around her waist. He mumbled something about Oxford looking quite splendid and Swati mumbled something about how the world always looked nice when one had one's arms around a woman. Mayank thought this was uncalled for but didn't let go of her waist.

On reaching his hall of residence, Mayank realized he had forgotten his code. He punched in variations on a four-digit theme: 5281, 1285 and 8215 but the door refused to budge. After five minutes, Mayank was about to give up and walk across the road to the Porter's Lodge to get help when the door swung open. Libby to the rescue. She had been walking around downstairs trying to find a light. She had an unlit candle in her hand. Would Mayank have a box of matches on him? Mayank hesitated for a second. A simple thought tiptoed across his mind. She does not offer me her cookies when I go to her room. Why should I share my light with her? He heard Swati thank her for letting them in. He felt her unfamiliar hand reach into his pocket with artificial familiarity. She fished around for the lighter, then handed it to Libby.

The first thing that Swati noticed when she entered Mayank's room was the CD player on the bed. 'Do you sleep with that thing?'

'I know,' laughed Mayank, 'yes, that's it's rightful place. I go to bed listening to my favourite album and I like waking up the same way. Mad, no?' He pressed play and a Leonard Cohen song came on. She threw her hands in the air, 'Oh, I looove Leonard Cohen.' Mayank opened a bottle of red wine. Swati said she was fine; she did not feel like drinking. She dug into the white thermocol box of chips, cheese and doner kebab which they had picked up from the kebab van on St. Giles. Mayank poured himself a glass and switched on the telly.

It wasn't that Mayank didn't want to have sex. He felt that Swati's aggression towards his music system was unnecessary. He lost interest in her the moment she turned to him and said in a sharp voice, 'Is that *thing* going to remain on the bed all night? Even when I am around?'

'Yes,' he had replied in an even tone that betrayed nothing. It was the kind of 'yes' that brooked no further discussion.

They did kiss for a while on the carpet but the fire inside Mayank had grown cold. Why did she have to be nasty about the one thing in the world that meant something to him. Cold heartless bitch. Didn't she realize that nothing else mattered . . . his parents, his life, his future—it was all bollocks, really. Of all the things in the world she had to find his CD player offensive. That poor, old, cute thing he had carried all the way from New Delhi in his hand luggage.

'You don't find me attractive?' asked Swati plaintively.

'No, it's not that,' said Mayank, 'just tired.'

'Well, I'm tired too,' said Swati pushing him away, looking for her clothes. 'Listen,' she said in a voice that concealed no hard feelings, 'if you don't mind can I crash here? I don't really care about the CD player if I'm sleeping. I'll walk back in the morning. It's just that I'm too tired to trudge back at this hour. Besides, you don't look in any shape to walk me back,' she concluded laughingly.

'Yeah, sure,' Mayank said listlessly, 'of course, you can stay for as long as you want. Let me make some space on the bed so you can sleep more comfortably.'

Mayank sat watching telly till late. He was careful not to turn the volume up too high. Swati had turned her back to him and the telly, and gone to sleep. As far as Mayank could tell she seemed comfortable, oblivious of her surroundings. He had finished the bottle of wine and was now drinking a can of Holsten Pilsner that he had found in the shared fridge in the kitchen outside. The Holsten did not belong to him. Was it a crime to consume a beer that belonged to somebody else? Mayank sipped on the beer and thought hard. He was going to replace it tomorrow first thing. That is if he managed to get up at all. He was aware that tomorrow-first-thing might very well not arrive before tomorrow evening.

He knew it was late because they were showing *Naked Elvis* on Channel 4. The show began with a man dressed up as Elvis. As the show progressed, Elvis gradually lost all his Elvisness apart from his shades and stick-on sideburns. The last segment featured him butt naked, grinding his hips, his limp manhood dangling precariously between his thighs.

As soon as the show finished, Mayank felt sick. He needed to throw up immediately. The reasons for his feeling nauseous were not clear. Was it the sight of the male organ, swinging like an emergency chain in an Indian railway compartment? Or was it just that he had had too much to drink?

He stumbled towards the vanity unit in the corner of the room, barely managing to reach it in time. He flung the door open, pulled the cord switch, leaned forward and aimed straight for the drain hole.

As a schoolboy, Mayank had always treaded middle ground. He was not a social disaster but at the same time he liked to maintain his distance from people and events. Maybe he had no choice in the matter. Maybe he was born with a congenital inability to immerse himself in the present.

This gap between his self and what the self experienced translated, in Mayank's thirteen-year-old mind, into a gap between his sense of self and the body that the self inhabited. The self and the body were separate entities, dwelling in mutually exclusive realms. This enabled him to observe the world around him and everything that it contained, including his own body, with a sense of detachment. His body could have been an apple lying on a table.

Every day when his parents went for their regulation evening walk, he would play with his body. He would strip to his underclothes and examine himself in the mirror. He would slip on his mother's bangles and anklets and rings, his palms sticky with fuzzy desire; he would stuff fluorescent tennis balls under his vest—the mere sight of these pretend breasts would leave him flushed and excited. He had developed a hearing as keen as a dog's. His ears were trained to wait for the thump-thump of feet ascending the staircase, the key turning in the Godrej lock.

A full ten minutes after barfing, Mayank stood in front of the mirror, his hands resting on the edge of the basin. His calm, untouched self sat regally on a throne like a benign raja, calmly observing and calculating the damages inflicted on his body— the bloodshot eyes, the runny nose, the burning in the solar plexus, the taste of sour vomit in the mouth. This calm self also noticed something else that wasn't part of his body. A small pouch stuffed with things lay on the flat top that surrounded the basin. The zipper was shut except for a small opening at one end. The oversized head of a toothbrush emerged ominously from this opening, like a naughty baby snake that wasn't supposed to be there in the first place. It was as if the snake had tried to slither out of the pouch and make a getaway, then changed its mind at the last minute when it realized that the world was a hostile place where snakes with poison in their fangs were feared but baby snakes—no matter how prickly their bristles—were dismissed as mere toothbrushes.

The pouch belonged to Swati. She had taken it out of her handbag because she wanted to brush her teeth before she went to bed. Mayank now unzipped it. He was thrilled to discover that it was full of her make-up stuff.

Mayank turned around to check on Swati. She still had her back towards him. Thank god for that. He could see her shoulders in all their bare and bony glory. Her knee-length, off-shoulder black dress lay abandoned on the carpet. Mayank tried but failed to resist temptation.

He undressed, slipped into the black dress. It was not easy but he managed. He remembered an old college friend telling him about how she had dressed her boyfriend up in a sari once, and discovered she found him sexiest that way. 'Insanely sexy' was the phrase she had used. Mayank felt insanely sexy in the smoky black dress. He'd harboured a secret crush on this friend for many years before she disappeared into sunny California with her sari-clad partner. He wished she could see him now.

Next, he took out Swati's mascara. He drew black circles around his eyes, rock 'n' roll style, as if he was going to a Kiss concert. Satisfied with the effect he had achieved he replaced it, fished out a stick of reddish-brown lip gloss. This he applied carefully, correctly, with the practised ease of a receptionist used to touching up her lips every half hour or so. He took off the tiny button earrings he was wearing and replaced them with long mango-shaped ones that swayed merrily, juicily, each time he shook his head. There were more discoveries along the way, like the clip-on nose ring which he happily clamped to his right nostril. Now he felt like a vamp in a Hindi soap. He tried to get into her stilettos but they were too small for him. Disappointed, but not wanting to accept defeat, he returned to the magical pouch that seemed to contain just about everything he would require on a desert island, an island where he could do whatever he felt like without fear of censure or ridicule.

A chunky bracelet of oxidized metal caught his eye. Extricating this bracelet was a delicate operation that involved disentangling it from various other pieces of jewellery floating around in the pouch—rings, necklaces, thin silver bangles. Every once in a while, Swati would turn around and change her position. But her eyes remained firmly shut. If she had seen him, she was certainly not saying anything. Initially, Mayank felt jittery each time she moved, but by now he was far too happy, too far gone, to care.

Mayank felt giggly. He surveyed himself in the mirror and fell in love with what he saw. His overarching, distant self congratulated itself at having wrought such heavenly transformation on both face and body. He walked up and down the room, swaying his hips. Instead of pulling his shoulders back, he let them hunch forward. He raised his warm, left shoulder and brought it to his cheek. He drew his forearms up, so that they were at right angles to his biceps, then let the wrists drop limp. He went back to the mirror. He worshipped what he saw.

People say that the past always catches up with you. An evening of reasonably heavy drinking caught up with Mayank at about two in the morning. He simply had to pee.

The urge had registered on Mayank's radar earlier but he had ignored it. In the excitement of trying on the off-shoulder dress and discovering the contents of the pouch, engrossed in the satisfaction of one urge, he had suppressed the voice of another equally important citizen of the urge world.

But urges are urges. They don't just go away. If unattended they only get bigger and badder.

Mayank poked his head out and monitored the situation. He was on the ground floor of the building. At one end of the passage lay the showers, the students' bar and the toilets. A staircase rose at the other end, leading to more rooms on the first floor, the floor where Libby lived.

Mayank searched for signs of light under the doors but found none. Everyone on his floor was asleep or at least pretending to. But, more worryingly, signs of life floated in from the bar. Mayank could make out drunken voices, the bang and rattle of table football. Stragglers at the bar often patronized the toilet in the passageway—the one Mayank wanted to use—because it was the nearest.

Mayank calculated. It would take him around twenty seconds to sprint to the toilet, thirty to relieve himself and another twenty to sprint back. A lot could happen in these seventy seconds. What if someone came in from the bar to use the toilet, just as Mayank was emerging from it? People might descend the first-floor staircase on their way to the computer room that lay beyond the bar. Students are natural insomniacs and compulsive e-mailers. Libby and Mayank had often bumped into each other in the computer room at fairly late hours.

But this is the thing about an urge. One can only deliberate up to a point. After that one just surrenders. Mayank opened the door further, then made a dash for it. He ran blindly, the dress restricting the easy movement of his thighs. Beads of sweat trickled down his forehead, smudging the big mascara circles he had drawn around his eyes. He shut the toilet door behind him. One-third of the mission was accomplished. Now for the piss, and the return sprint. Mayank lifted his dress and released a jet of urine into the WC.

Mayank had no intentions of staying in the toilet longer than the act required. He was not going to sit around in that deathly white cubicle contemplating the risk factor. He was going to run and hope for the best. He opened the door. There was nobody outside. The door that led to the bar was shut although there were still people on the other side.

Mayank scampered down the passage on tiptoe. He must have been two doors away from his room when he heard the bar door creak open. He had no option but to keep running. They were behind him now. It was best he did not turn around to see who it was. That would give his identity away.

He reached his door but did not turn around to face it. Instead he stopped dead in his tracks, his body not facing the panel but at right angles to it. He turned the knob, pushed the door with his right shoulder. Swati was still sleeping. Almost immediately Mayank heard the group go past. They were talking excitedly amongst themselves. Mayank was too breathless and terrified to listen.

He knew they had seen him but only from the back. He hoped they thought it was a girl spending the night in his room, not him dressed up as a girl. He hoped they were drunk and self-absorbed; maybe they hadn't even noticed that there was someone in front of them. He looked down at his legs and wished they were not so hairy. He wondered how Swati could sleep so soundly in a strange bed.

The Farewell

On the last day of school, there was a fight. No one quite knows what happened. One minute we were standing in neat rows, the next there was pandemonium. The girls huddled together on the stage of the auditorium, like nuns in a besieged convent, while the boys had it out on the floor. The teachers who tried to intervene got beaten up. A group of boys drove around the dusty cricket field in an open Jeep, firing shots into the air. It wasn't clear whether this was being done in provocation or celebration. Mayank Luthra, always a loner, stood in a corner of the auditorium, breaking plates. Gingerly he picked up each plate with both hands, then raised it above his head as if offering prayers to the sun god, before finally letting it crash to the floor. He went through two entire stacks, both eyes shut tight, a picture of contemplative aggression in a gallery of flying fists.

By eleven in the morning, it was clear that the farewell was not going to last till the afternoon as planned. The plates were all smashed, the cola stolen. I cycled back home to pack in an extra two hours of cable TV. MTV had just come to

Allahabad with its drop-your-sideburns ads and all-American programming. The Pearl Jam-obsessed Danny McGill was its star VJ. When I switched on the family's black and white television set, Eddie Vedder was growling, 'I am alive' into a microphone. Then, in what looked to be a desperate attempt to drive a point home, Vedder chucked the mike and dived into the crowd. To my seventeen-year-old self, just back from the failed farewell at Boys' High School, this seemed to confirm a growing suspicion—that the world was chaos and anarchy the way forward.

Two years earlier, my school—an all boys' grind established more than a hundred years ago—had turned co-ed. 'I've decided to throw some roses among the thorns,' declared Frederic DeSouza, the principal, at our first co-ed assembly.

I promptly fell in love. Thorny, bespectacled me fell in love with rosy, anorexic Rachna. She had matchsticks for legs and long, very long hair.

I discovered New Kids on the Block and yellow Digene. I bought an Archies card (ten clocks displayed on the front and inside the punchline: 'It's time we got together') and gave it to Rachna between the covers of an accounting register.

Rachna responded by refusing to acknowledge my presence in class. I was desperate. Then one day she passed me a note: *Come for the soccer match in the evening.*

It's 12 C vs 12 A. I arrive in a white Smash T-shirt, light blue Wranglers and a rexine belt studded with stars. We say hello and shut up for another hour. Afterwards, she says goodbye and leaves with her girlfriends. Minutes later, I am surrounded by three guys. They have country pistols. 'Light-eyed lover boy, *kanja deewana*,' they tell me, 'get off her trail or else . . .'

In the next few days, I discover a thing or two about dating in Allahabad. Want girl? Get 'backing'. Whose backing? Of the Hindi-medium types—the kind who've been flunking class 9 for the last five years. They carry arms, they have scars, they have the lingo. A typically violent east UP lingo where women are always whores (*chinar*) and sex is always about robbing virginity (*seal todna*).

The English-medium kids need the Hindi-medium goons. The latter too need the former—they want to be seen with the cooler English-speaking boys. In the evenings, they form groups and hang out outside downtown soft-drink booths.

I want to be able to speak to Rachna freely but can't. After the soccer rendezvous, the entire town is out to get me. Rachna and I exchange smiles in class and at the school gate, but that's about it. I am shit scared; she is totally confused. I have a vague idea that I shouldn't let on that I am shit scared. Girls like brave men. Besides, what idea could this dainty little girl possibly have about the big, bad world of gangs, motorbikes and bicycle chains?

One morning, just before assembly, Gaurav Arora, the school jock, strolls over to where I am standing. He is reputed to have a way with girls. Gaurav offers some friendly advice: 'Anand Mishra knows about your date. He's really pissed off.

Rachna is his *maal*. He's coming at recess to break your bones. At least that's what he told me. Take my advice, buddy. Go home right now, because as far as I can see you have no backing.' I ponder over his suggestion for a minute, then decide against leaving the school campus. If girls like brave men, then this is my moment. I will not run away. I will be brave.

Mishra arrives with his gang at the appointed hour. He is twice my size and flaunts a thumb-sized scar on his right cheek. He is in third-year BCom. I am summoned to the canteen: 'Mishra wants to see you.' It turns out that's all he wants to do. When face to face, he stares at me unsmilingly, then asks me to leave.

The next day, in the library period, Rachna invites me to sit next to her. I hesitate for a moment. I know there are spies in our class. Mishra will get to know immediately. 'Come here, sit with me,' repeats Rachna. Her hair smells of lemon, her hands are tiny and pretty, her eyes are lined with kohl—I allow myself to be seduced. We open a *Sportstar* and have our first proper conversation. 'Why did you have to pass a card? Couldn't you have just said it . . . like with your mouth?'

'If you don't like my card you are most welcome to return it.'

There is a pause in the conversation. She decides to overlook my offer. 'I heard Anand Mishra came to school yesterday,' she giggles. I look up from the *Sportstar*, an expression of surprise on my face. 'What did he say?' I don't reply. 'If you want I will have a word with him,' she offers, and then, without waiting for a reply, she decides the matter for me. 'In fact, I *will* have a word with him. He won't touch you.

You don't worry. Call me in the evening.' I dig out the school diary from my bag and write down her number. The bell goes. While we are walking out, Rachna turns to me and says, 'That card. You know what? You bought it from my shop. The stock came in from Delhi on Saturday. I put it on the display rack on Monday morning.'

The librarian is staring at us. She's got a squarish face and an oily nose. One can sense her mind is in turmoil. She feels the world is coming to a premature and violent end. Her gaze latches on to our backs like a fish hook and refuses to let go even when we are back in our dingy and damp classroom.

I graduate to calling Rachna up every evening at 5. I have *her* backing. I never graduate to taking her to the *tila*, which is a desolate mound on the outskirts of town, at the very edge of the cantonment, overlooking mustard fields. Serious couples come here to plot elopement and discover the sense of touch. There is no place for them on the main drag. They exist on the fringes, away from prying eyes.

I call Rachna every day after my accounts tuition. There is no phone at home so I bicycle down to Kohinoor Chemist in Civil Lines. In the age of the PCO, he is one of the last to have a black, one-rupee slot phone. Drop a one-rupee coin and talk for as long as you like. I usually talk for around three quarters of an hour, then go home. The Babri Masjid has been brought down in Ayodhya. There have been riots across the country. Allahabad is 'tense but under control'. Like my adolescent dick. My parents want me home before sundown.

Anand Mishra was a regular visitor to school, but thankfully I was no longer his centre of attention. He had other enemies to rough up, other battles to fight, other girls to chase. I never asked Rachna about what she'd told him but it certainly had its desired effect. Each time he bumped into me he would insist on a brotherly hug. He would pat me on the back forcefully and offer me his backing: 'Hero, go after any girl in Allahabad, *madarchod koi bhi ladki ho*, I will make sure no one touches you. *Aa jaye koi bhi mai ka lal, uski bahin ke bur mein* . . . You really like Rachna, don't you? Just remember one thing: she's a fucking fireball.'

Once, he took me home with him. He and his cronies were watching porn films on video. Black man, white woman, grainy print. After an hour, Mishra seemed to tire of the incessant fucking. *'Abey bas kar, Kaloo, kitna chodega?'* he laughed, switching off the VCR. He said he wanted me to see a bit of his favourite film, a football saga called *Hip Hip Hurray*. Everyone in school had seen it and so had I. It had run to packed houses at Plaza. I had completely forgotten the scene he showed me. Raj Kiran is a teacher, freshly arrived in a small-town college. Some student goons feel that he is getting too fresh too quick with another teacher who is extremely beautiful, and whom they all secretly adore.

One night one of the students knocks on his door and delivers a threat: 'Teacher, *yeh Bambai nahi hain, yahaan laundiyabaji nahin chalegi.*' This, Mishra told me, was one of the best scenes in the film. Explaining himself, he said, 'Delivering threats is an art. Your eyes, your tone of voice, your body language, everything has to be just right. One wrong step and the other person will dismiss you as a cunt. And in life, brother, you cannot afford to be called a cunt. Everyone, yes, everyone in Allahabad knows who I am and respects me. No motherfucker dare touch me. There's a reason for this.'

When I was about to leave, Mishra asked me if I could help him out with something. 'How can I ever be of any help to you?' I joked nervously. 'There is this girl,' he said, 'and I want to make her a proposal. I've got this card. You know how these St Mary's girls are: all these English types. I want you to take this card and write some nice poetries in it in your own handwriting. I'll be coming to school tomorrow. That Kamlesh fellow has grown too big for his boots. The bastard was staring at me yesterday. No one holds my gaze. Ever. I'll pick up the card from you, then sort him out.'

One year down the line, Mishra disappeared. Rumour was that he was in love with a Muslim girl. Both the families were united in their mission: find their wards and murder them. Mishra and his lover, everyone said, had gone underground in Nepal.

Nazneen Khan, who was said to be related to Salman Khan, the film star, was friends with Sameera, the girl who had eloped. One evening, over a vanilla milkshake at Hotstuff, she told me that she had heard from Sameera. The two were in Calcutta, but they wouldn't be there for long. They were on the run. Both sets of parents were serious about killing their children. There were rumours in Allahabad that the girl was pregnant and had had an abortion. Nazneen was disconcertingly deadpan and non-judgemental about the whole affair. The couple was doing what they had to do; the parents were doing what they were supposed to do. At the end of the day, it was a private matter.

The day after our conversation, the vice principal had a quiet word with Nazneen. 'You have been seen in town, sitting in restaurants, talking to boys. The reputation of the school is at stake. Just don't, okay?'

I was next in line. Jha, the vice princi, grabbed hold of my tie—which hung lose around my neck in accepted senior-school style—and slid the knot up rather vigorously. 'And you,' he muttered, 'you better concentrate on your studies. Okay?'

'Okay.'

Almost a year had passed since the Rachna-Archies card-Mishra incident. This was my final year at school. Exactly nine months to the farewell and then I was out of here.

Relationships in Allahabad seldom went beyond phone conversations. I had had my fill of these as far as Rachna was concerned. Things could only go further if your family owned a motor spare parts shop and a Maruti 800. We owned neither. Rachna knew several such characters and had been seen in Jhusi, in an air-conditioned Maruti parked on the banks of the Ganges.

I myself was now besotted with a girl called Divya who had joined school in class 11. She had silky black hair, which she wore short, and sad brown eyes like a cocker spaniel. Her face was dotted with pimples. She was a committed NCC cadet. Her walk was a fetching combination of army erectness and girlie bum-swaying. After an afternoon of disciplined marching, she would walk back to the cycle stand, her face the colour of a tomato, the epaulettes on her khaki shirt hanging loose.

This year my backing came from two sources: Nazneen Khan and Karan. Nazneen had invested in six garish rakhis on Raksha Bandhan. She had strategically tied these on the wrists of six school louts who had been making passes at her. Now they were her protectors. And, by proxy, they became my protectors too.

I had also decided to strike out on my own. At a Bollywood-style dance competition called Anubhav '93, organized at the Sangeet Samiti, I met Karan. I was wearing a big, fat gangsta pendant around my neck. I wore it outside my T-shirt, where it hung at around navel level, glinting proudly in the sun. This caught Karan's eye. He walked over to me and introduced himself. He said he liked my style.

I watched the dance competition sitting with Karan's gang. He was squabbling with his girlfriend so we didn't get a chance to talk much that afternoon. But each time we met in Civil Lines at Osho's STD booth, he would ask me how things were and if I needed any help.

My self-image had undergone a change in the last year or so. I no longer thought of myself as the self-sufficient introvert who liked doing things on his own. I had realized that if you were in an east UP town, and were mildly ambitious, you certainly needed 'help'. It would be foolish to turn it down. As it turned out, I soon needed help with Divya.

Things were going great with her. She gave me a big bar

of Cadbury's and a 'best friend' card on my birthday. This was certainly an improvement on Rachna. On the Annual Prize Day in school, we even managed a finger shake through a slat in the grill. I was standing in the corridor waiting to collect my prizes; she was outside, performing her prefectorial duties: getting the junior prizewinners to stand straight and still. I could not call at her place because, as she told me, her brother had just eloped with a girl and her parents were very upset. If they found out now that a boy was calling their home and asking for her, they might not survive the double shock. My parents still did not have a phone, so I made an arrangement with my classmates, Ravi and Rishi Gupta. They were twins and lived in a neighbourhood not too far from mine.

I would go to their place under the pretext of doing 'joint studies'. We would keep the cordless with us. Divya would call twice; the first time she would let the phone ring a couple of times, then cut the line. The second call would follow exactly a minute later.

We never let it go beyond the first ring because Mrs Gupta was a light sleeper and an instinctive slapper. During our conversations, Divya never ceased to remind me of my class topper status. 'You always do well in exams,' she would say good-naturedly. 'You should concentrate on your books, building a career.'

Divya and I had a friend in common: Sankalp. Sankalp and I were together in middle school. Then he flunked, and kept flunking. But we had been good friends. Our school did not have organized games in the recess, but this doesn't mean we did not have team sports. It was a big school; every boy worth his salt was part of a team. There was nothing official about it.

Your ability to put a team together and find teams to play with depended on your initiative, persuasive skills and charisma. I had a team of my own: the Allahabad Wings. Our sport was soccer and Sankalp our star goalie. Instead of a proper soccer ball, we played with a cricket-sized one made of cork. We played wearing our regular Naughty Boy shoes; needless to say, tackles could be very painful.

It turned out that Divya and Sankalp lived in the same neighbourhood. She had been coaching him every single day and under her tutelage Sankalp had been making progress. He had also fallen for her.

One rainy afternoon after school, I found myself surrounded yet again. There was a black Kawasaki Bajaj, a red Ind Suzuki and a silver-grey Hero Honda. The guy on the KB delivered the message: '*Sankalp ka dil Divya par aa gaya hai. Baki to tum jaante hi ho.*'

I nodded my head but was noncommittal. They suggested I nip it in the bud and promised to return next week. In the evening I went to Osho's STD looking for Karan. I hadn't seen him for almost a fortnight now. There was no one at the STD except for Osho, the owner. 'Haven't you heard?' he said, 'Karan's left arm was blown off in a crude bomb attack. Vicky Wadhwa's men. His parents have taken him to Delhi.'

The next morning, before classes for the day had begun, Divya walked up to me and called the whole thing off: 'I won't be able to speak to you any more. Do not try and call me, don't expect any calls from me. In school you will pretend that I don't exist. Goodbye.'

After this incident I was heartbroken. I vowed never to fall in love. I also became a professional go-between. My standard charge was two Pepsis for every card passed. The Pepsis had to be paid for in advance.

This was a market just waiting to be tapped. Allahabad was full of schoolboys who had the requisite backing but possessed neither the courage nor the language skills to get their message across. At Flynn's Coaching Centre I would take on the responsibility—and risk—of passing other people's cards. The boys would hide behind a bush while I stopped Luna after Luna: 'Aseem has sent this for you. Please accept this. He's a really nice boy.' The message I took back to the boys, nine times out of ten, was: 'I am not that kind of girl. I am not interested in such activities. Will you please stop blocking my way?' I did this with a certain cold-bloodedness. The heartache wasn't mine, and, besides, I had already been paid in calories.

Twelve years later I bump into Gaurav Arora outside El Chico restaurant. He has put on weight, has an air of prosperity. The jock has become a full-fledged businessman. He tells me about his recent Goa trip: '*Kya* sex *ladkiya thi, bhai saab.*' As for Allahabad, what can he say? It's a village.

It's not so bad, I say, consoling him. Civil Lines has changed. There is a lot more neon, and a lot more street children. I point out the new Sony showroom, the broadband Internet cafés, the restaurant that serves passable Italian food. 'Sure,' he says, 'you're right. It's not that things haven't changed. The spaghetti at that Italian place is not bad.'

He asks me if I am married.

'No.'

'Hey, you know what happened to that *chinar* you were in love with, that Rachna chick? She went to Delhi and settled there. We rarely saw her here. Then, last month, I saw this black and white photograph in a Hindi magazine. The caption read: Six call girls arrested in Delhi. Although the girls were covering their faces with their hands, I could make out that one of them was Rachna. I swear it was Rachna. I am an Allahabadi: I can recognize one when I see one.'

'But if they were covering their faces, you really can't be sure it was her, can you?'

'Sure? What are you talking about, yaar, all whores, bhaiya, A-1 whores, take it from me. Everyone knows.'

Arora's cellphone went off somewhere on his body. He dug out a fancy Sony Ericsson handset.

'Hi, Namrata,' he whispered in English, 'I am with a friend. I'll just call you back.'

'I am getting married next month, Lucknow girl, my bua's choice,' he informs me stuffing the phone back into his front pocket. 'Just enjoying my courtship period.'

The Other Evening

Mullaji—the owner of a belly the size of a pumpkin, and several petty businesses, including a butcher's shop—is the local entrepreneur of Okhla Basti. It was here, at his small butcher's shack, that we first met. Except that then, instead of raw meat, Mullaji was into selling biryani. I would drop by at Nasir bhai's to pick up a tola or two of ganja and would invariably succumb to the temptation of a chillum. So it happened one time that I had smoked plenty—I can't quite remember how many chillums, and had felt very hungry afterwards. And it was while eating in Mullaji's shack that I met Roxy, the pimp. After a plateful of biryani, I shared another chillum with Roxy, who had, in the meantime, explained to me that he preferred his friends to call him Ahmad. I wasn't too sure how I'd become his friend, but, then, most people at Mullaji's had passed through Nasir bhai's smoking den; they tended to be in a generous mood. At some point in the conversation, Ahmad promised me a girl; I gave him my address, fixed a time for the next day and left. The following morning I had completely forgotten about the encounter, so when Roxy turned up in the evening I was a little surprised and even scared.

At first I didn't believe it. A pimp is just not supposed to behave this way. A nondescript, sallow youth, casually draped over my landlady's ornate iron gate, shouting, almost screaming, *'Aaa ke le ja,'*—loud enough for old Mrs Khosla, two houses down to the left, to look up from her gardening, her eyes all scrunched up like paper balls. Wouldn't he want to be discreet—if not for my, then for his own sake?

Let's not forget the dog downstairs (I poisoned him a few weeks later, but that's another story). The insecure rat of a Pomeranian—a supposedly unwanted Valentine's Day present for the landlady's daughter—had been abandoned with Devinder, the manservant, who lived in the garage below my room. Within weeks of the dog's arrival, Devinder imported his entire family from his village: a tall and striking-looking wife, two young sons, and a daughter who usually hung around the staircase—always a pink ribbon in her hair—looking rather lost and homesick. Once, on a rainy afternoon, when I lay wasted after a night of heavy drinking, complicated by a near-fatal bout of food poisoning, Devinder's daughter arrived at my doorstep with a motichoor laddu. It turned out that while I lay wheezing and croaking, Devinder's woman had given birth to a baby daughter, right there in the garage. 'Is there a dai there?' I asked the little girl. She shook her head. I figured Devinder must have rolled up his sleeves for this one.

When the pimp shouted my name, the Pom, who stayed tied to the open garage door, exploded with fury, which—her lunge being thwarted by the shortest of leashes—manifested itself in vigorous barking; and, then, as if the bell had gone off for the school assembly, the three children neatly arranged themselves, in descending order of height, at the garage door. The Pom continued to lunge, looking like a plane during take-off, stuck perennially to the runway at a 45-degree angle.

Once the two were in my room, I got a chance to have a closer look. The girl was of medium height—a few inches shorter than me—and mildly cock-eyed. Her hair was parted sideways and a silver nose ring glistened in her right nostril. She wore cheap perfume, chipped red nail polish and flared trousers, punched with aluminium-rimmed zeroes. A tight, full-sleeved, acrylic blouse covered what seemed to be ample breasts. One of her front teeth was chipped vertically. She had an open, warm smile despite the offending tooth.

It so happened that, just at that moment, a friend of mine, Soumik, decided to drop by. To be honest I was a trifle embarrassed. And worried. This friend was not the trustworthy sort. Or let's put it this way—while he would jump into swirling waters to save you if you were drowning, there was no guarantee that he would not clobber you to death once you were safe and dry on the shore. It must have taken him exactly three seconds to figure out what was going on. He turned to me with a bemused expression and asked: How much are you paying for her? Well, I replied, I haven't really figured it out but I don't particularly like the way she looks. At this he made a grand gesture with his right hand, a gesture that said: Just lie back and let me take care of all this.

I remember yielding rather reluctantly, and thinking: If he can save me a few hundred rupees, why not?

Did you get her through the health club listings?

No.

Should've asked me, man. Anyway . . . said Soumik, his hands rising and falling, cutting intricate patterns in the air, doing most of the talking again.

The girl was obviously hassled by the bargaining. She kept telling the pimp that there was no point, and that they should leave at once. Her voice, I noticed, was unassuming; her tone self-deprecating.

In five minutes, Soumik had bargained her price down by a thousand rupees. You really serious about this, are you? Expecting us to pay two grand for this piece of crap, he said, his tone incredulous, his gaze flickering from the pimp to the girl and back. She looked like she would burst into tears. But there are two of you, said the pimp in an uncertain voice. So what, said Soumik, we're doing her a favour.

What? The two of us? Since when did you become a part of this, boss? I protested. Soumik seemed irritated. Look, he said, trying to sound reasonable, why can't you be a little more flexible? And then, sounding more and more like a father speaking to an obstinate son, he proposed a deal: Let's go fifty-fifty on this. I'll do her in the loo. By now I was angry, almost seething. No, Soumik, I said, in as calm and steady a voice as possible, I'm not sharing her with anyone. Let that be absolutely clear.

I walked to the cupboard and took out a thousand rupees in cash. It was money I could ill afford to spend, but the events of the last few days had shaped up such that I didn't much care about anything really. I stuffed ten hundred-rupee notes into Roxy's hands, which, I noticed, were surprisingly well-manicured. He wanted extra money for the auto ride back; I gave him another fifty. He mumbled for some more; I stomped

my foot like a child and ordered everyone—except the girl—
out. Before Soumik could give me a hurt look I had banged the
door shut.

So here we are, the two of us, locked inside my room. My tiny
bed-sit which overlooks a service lane on one side, and a small,
decrepit park on the other. I sit on a chair made of cane and
rope; Pooja takes the chatai, cross-legged. I put the big
fluorescent light off and turn on the table lamp. The light falls
on her face from behind, lighting up half of it. She looks like
a witch, I think. I walk to the fridge and get myself a Kingfisher.
I drink straight from the bottle.

An awkward silence descends on the room. I take a sip of
the beer and try and think of something to say.

Do you want a drink?

No, she says, shaking her head. She does not look at me.
Instead, she runs a finger around the edges of a diamond-
shaped pattern on the chatai. I stare at the bottle in my hand.

When I look up she is flipping through a magazine. An
issue of *Cosmopolitan* which has an old schoolmate of mine,
Michelle, on the cover. Michelle and I were together when we
were fourteen. She was incredibly pretty even then, so beautiful
that I never had the courage to talk to her.

Pooja is walking around by now. She looks at the books
on my shelf, the CDs on the table, and then, turning to me,
exclaims: But they are all in English! I nod my head, confused
by her tone of voice, not sure if I should apologize.

Are you and your friend from abroad? she asks, picking up a Pulp CD.

It's a question I am asked often. I was once chased in Connaught Place by a man shouting, Money change? Young boys? Manali Cream? I'll always remember him as some sort of an illegitimate supermarket on wheels. Pooja, like most people, seems surprised, even disappointed, on learning of my native origins.

My beer is finished by now. I get up to get another. She is standing next to my chair, looking at the books again. I brush against her deliberately. She looks at her watch.

Are you sure you don't want a drink? I ask again.

She turns around and smiles at me: How much *do* you drink? Then, without waiting for an answer, she says: My boyfriend Raj drinks quite a bit. Especially, when he is not in a good mood. She finds this funny and bursts into giggles. Anyway, what do you have apart from beer? Momentarily unsettled by the mention of a boyfriend, I stare at her blankly. What else do you have to drink apart from beer, silly? she repeats, laughing for the first time since she stepped into the room.

Some gin and some vodka, I state blandly. She wants to see the bottles. I fetch them from the top of the refrigerator. Now she wants to smell the booze. I open both bottles and she brings the mouth of each to her nose, gingerly, gracefully, as if she is smelling carnations. Having decided on the gin, she demands a glass and some water. I give her the glass; she fixes herself a stiff one. I find the 5 litre Bisleri dispenser and pour some water into the tumbler. She laughs at the size of the dispenser—it's the size of a bucket—and comments on how absurd it looks in comparison to the glass. She gulps the drink down in one go. She asks for a repeat and gulps that down as well. Then she goes back to the magazine with Michelle on the cover. I return to the chair and start rolling a joint.

What's that? she asks, suddenly sounding very serious and proper.

Ganja. You are most welcome to have some.

She refuses. I light the joint, lean back, and ask if Raj smokes as well.

No, he doesn't, says Pooja, turning a page in the magazine.

Is the guy who brought you here Raj?

She is clearly bemused by the suggestion. Raj, she says, is not a skinny wimp like the tout. He is tall and handsome and has broad shoulders.

I wonder if Raj really exists or is a mere invention, an imagined saviour, a useful idea.

Meanwhile, Pooja, her tongue loosened by the alcohol, continues talking. She tells me Raj is going to marry her in two months' time. That's also when she plans to stop whoring and get a decent job.

I ask if she has been doing this for long and she says, No, not for too long, maybe a year. Then, she turns the question on me: Why do you ask me that? Do I not look like I'm in this line? She sounds worried. I hurriedly reassure her: No, no, of course you do.

She shows me her left palm. There, just where the lifeline meets the fateline, I see the name 'Raj' scribbled in English with a blue ballpen. Raj, she says, is always with her, wherever she goes.

Do you think he is here right now? I ask, a hint of mischief in my voice.

She looks me in the eye and says, Yes. Right here.

Her lips are cracked and crimson with lipstick and congealed blood. I kiss her just below, on her chin. For a moment I remain still, breathing in her cheap perfume and talc. Then, slowly, I pull up her acrylic blouse. It reveals a pair of brown tits, unusually soft and buttery, the left one sporting a black birthmark the shape of an almond. She arches her back and moans; I am convinced she is pretending.

Her back is as smooth as her hands are rough. Rough like I imagine a peasant's would be. She cries out in surprise when she feels mine—so smooth, she says, and mine so . . . Her voice trails away and she shakes her head in disgust. She seems to be rebuking herself. I kiss her from the nape of her neck to the base of her spine. I ask her to slap me. She refuses: How can I slap you, just like that? She cups my face in her palms and kisses my forehead. No . . . no, hit me, I like it, I protest. She gives me a confused look, pushes me away for a second and then draws me back to her breasts. I kiss her all over the face but again avoid the lips.

Her eyes drift to a necklace hanging on the wall next to the bookshelf: You must have lots of girlfriends. I say I never had too many; anyway, there are none at the moment. The necklace on the wall—well, that belongs to a previous girlfriend, someone with whom I had a five-year relationship and who ended up sleeping with another man. Some geezer she met on ICQ.

So you are heartbroken, she says. She sounds relieved. I also had my heart broken once, she offers by way of consolation, rather shyly, her head cocked to one side, her eyes looking into the distance. But the first one is always the toughest, she concludes, and, then, in a firm voice: Bas, no more, have to go. I hug her tightly; she keeps smiling and shaking her head as if something is worrying her. I beg her not to leave. Ever. I feel a curious drowsiness creeping up my spine, clutching at my lungs, tugging at my eyelids.

She looks at her watch and says she has to. She is late in any case—I have spent too much time talking. She has more business to attend to.

I stifle a pang of jealousy.

Can you give me some money for the auto? She is standing at the door, ready to leave.

I gave some to that fellow who came with you.

But that was for him.

I feel she is trying to rip me off, just like an auto guy.

She asks if I'm going to call for her again. I say maybe but I have no money. She mumbles something about the price being anyway quite low. I ask if thirty rupees will be sufficient for the ride back but hand her a crisp fifty. She wants to know where she can find an auto. An emotion, akin to raw fear, overwhelms me and makes me wobbly at the knees. I give her directions to the auto stand: turn left out of the gate, go straight down, hit the nala, turn left again, take the first right, down the bridge, over the nala, all the way to the flyover— you should find some rickshaws there. I think she wants me to walk her there. But she's not your lover, I tell myself. Besides, her clothes advertise the fact she is a whore; I shouldn't be seen with her. Especially at night, when car headlights capture you at your most vulnerable, and wallop you with their beams.

The Wrist

It all began with a late night phone conversation when she told him she liked Abhishek Bachchan's shoulders. That was just the beginning. She also told him about other parts of a man's body that she had found sexy in the past—Salman Khan's back, a South American tennis player's fit thigh, a labourer's sweaty arms as he laid tiles on a sloping roof. But it was the wrist that really got to Ravi. The dark, sweaty, muscular wrist and veiny hand clutching a bus handrail in Bangalore. She had found *that* sexy. When she said this Ravi couldn't help but look at his own instinctively—they were pretty and slender and bony, like his first girlfriend's.

Ravi and Abha had known each other for three years—they'd been seeing each other for the last two. They'd met at a book launch in Delhi. Her book launch. He had gone along with his then girlfriend, a reporter with a TV channel. Abha wore a blue Fabindia kurta and sat signing copies of her book, *A Lost Childhood: Twelve Stories of Abuse*, a stern expression on her face. In fact, it was the sternness that had appealed to Ravi, fresh with an MBA from an Australian university, and now working for a cosmetics company. Abha was intuitive, outspoken, always willing to lay into the Indian middle-class. The antipathy was crucial to her identity. On their first date she informed him that she liked to keep her nails short and neat. On the second, they fucked. 'Please be gentle with me,' she had said to him in a wailing voice, 'I'm just a simple, small town girl.'

Opposites attract they say, but in this case it didn't work out. Over the two years they had been living in, Abha had had blackouts, seizures, fainting fits, crying fits, panic attacks. She had disappeared from the house for days after a fight only to return home a week later, still hysterical but reasonably healthy. Ravi developed a bald patch and spent all his time arranging empty Red Riband halves in straight lines under the kitchen sink. He was sacked for reeking of alcohol at work. He became capricious, irritable, maudlin; he coughed, retched, threw up phlegm, walked the streets whispering into imaginary handsets.

This time when Abha disappeared after a fight, Ravi decided to disappear as well. He came to Dehra Dun and found himself a dormitory. It was a town he had been to school in, and where his mother still lived. One day, he called Abha in Delhi on a whim. To his surprise he got her. She was back in front of the TV, eating Haldiram's Nutcrackers and watching Ekta Kapoor's nasty soaps. She wanted to know where he was. Then she told him about a prize she had been recently awarded—she was off to Paris in a month's time. Ravi mumbled his congratulations. Then, suddenly, Abha's voice sounded distracted. 'Abhishek Bachchan is on *Koffee with Karan*,' Abha said, 'let me just call you back.'

Ravi sat in his room pressing digits on his mobile phone. He didn't like waiting. He tore a page out of a small pad and wrote a note to his mother. 'Hi Ma. All is well. Been very busy working though I am thinking of changing jobs. Abha and I are also planning to have our first baby. We'll both come to Dehra one of these weekends. Do take care, Ravi.'

I must go to an Internet café tomorrow and key this in first thing, he told himself. He often wrote mental memos to himself. Ever since he could remember, Ravi was good at taking the first step but not the successive ones. Maybe he lacked what the entire Indian cricket team supposedly lacked— the killer instinct. He would buy his partner a present, then keep it in his drawer; he would write a letter but never get down to posting it; he would manage to get a woman in the sack, then fail to get it up.

The phone rings. It's Abha. 'Hi, sorry I took a bit getting back. Thought I'd check my mail before calling you.' They are talking normally. They do this sometimes—pretend things are okay when they are not. In hate they become accomplices. 'The French called to say that everything's in the post—details of ticket and hotel reservations, maps, phone numbers. It should be here in four or five days. They've really been very nice. The award ceremony is on the fourteenth.'

Abha is in a talkative mood. Ravi, on the other hand, feels closed in, clammed up, spirally. He needs to jack off. Abha has just finished watching *Koffee with Karan*—she can't stop talking about Abhishek. 'You once said,' says Abha taking issue, 'that men are more visual than women—they respond more to visual stimuli. Not true.' She talks about shoulders, backs and thighs. She talks about the wrist on the bus, 'I never saw this man's face but it was the sexiest male wrist I ever saw.'

Ravi walks around the dormitory. There is no one around. He has all twelve bunk beds to himself—six of them covered with stained white bed sheets. Naked mattresses adorn the other six. A thin film of dust carpets the red floor—nothing unpleasant, just a fingernail coating, a five o'clock shadow as opposed to a full beard.

The walls are thin. The ceiling looks like it's made of bullet-holed cork. There is a battered Sharp television set which works if you bang it hard with a clenched fist. Mirrors hang on opposite walls adding a semblance of depth to, what is at heart, a small and narrow room.

Ravi cannot sleep. Strangers lie in wait, lurk in the bylanes of his mind, waiting to pounce on and strike down any genuine emotion like warmth, or a genuine attitude like forgiveness, that dares walk down the main drag. He thinks he can hear people talking somewhere. He tries to eavesdrop on the conversation but can only hear muffled sounds.

Ravi strips to his underclothes and paces the floor. It's early April. The nights still have a chill in Dehra Dun. While walking he catches a glimpse of his slender boyish body in one of the mirrors. He looks around the dorm and remembers the community showers at boarding school. He remembers the naked bodies becoming bigger and more muscular as each week passed by; the girls lusting after those glorious torsos— Ravi, not on any sports team, at the receiving end of a series of rotten rejections.

He chooses a bunk bed and lies down on his back. He has left one light on. He observes the ornate shade, the head of the bulb peeping nervously out of its floral foreskin. Off-white moths circle endlessly, give furtive kisses, then fall to the ground and die as abruptly as they were born.

Ravi shuts his eyes. He finds the spaces under his eyelids suffused with a dusky orange twilight. Ravi hasn't noticed yet but there is a man lying on the bunk bed above his own. He has been lying there for hours.

Now, as Ravi tosses and turns, the man raises himself, dangles his legs over the edge. Ravi can see the outlines of his legs but not the details. Even when he descends Ravi can't see him clearly. Although the outline suggests that the man is big, the bulk of his form is filled with darkness.

Ravi, half-scared, half-excited, inspects this muscular darkness that has carved a niche for itself in the homogeneous orange light. The man walks towards Ravi, naked except for a pair of boots. 'This cannot be an apparition,' Ravi, now sitting upright, tells himself, 'aren't apparitions supposed to be soundless?'

The man barks an order, 'Strip and lie face down on the bed. Do not move.' He has a deep bass voice, like a low growl. It exudes authority, certainty; it's a voice that is used to being listened to and obeyed.

Ravi has no choice. He can feel his free will dissipate. He does as he is told.

The man sits astride Ravi's buttocks and straps his wrists and ankles to the corners of the bed. Ravi can sense the weight and touch of his naked buttocks on his own. He can also sense a temperature difference—his is icy cold while the man's seem to burn with an unnatural heat.

The man lies on top of him crushing him under his weight. Ravi can feel his matchstick arms and legs dissolve, merge into the pillars the giant has for limbs; he feels the man's heavy breath on his neck, his stubble against his ears, his broad hairy chest tickling his back.

The apparition grinds his hips slowly, tightly, all the while pressing into Ravi's buttocks. He doesn't enter but shafts his swollen cock up and down the downy crevice between Ravi's flat cheeks.

The man comes in violent spurts. Ravi feels like he just finished an hour-long tumble dry cycle, like a jet plane whizzed past inches from his nose.

He feels the man rubbing semen all over him, massaging his arse with the fresh grease, the thick wet fingers groping for his arsehole. And then, the final intimate touches—a dab of semen on each of his earlobes, and his nose. They lie like that for hours—Ravi face down on the bed, the man on top of him, not saying anything. The man's arms lie on either side of his neck, rough and inert, like a pair of alligators. If Ravi turns his head a little he can see the man's wrist. It's hairy, muscular, powerful. It's the kind of wrist that fires machine guns and steers trucks with hydraulic brakes. It's the kind of wrist, Ravi tells himself, that commits no double faults. It's the kind of wrist which, in case the owner ever found himself in a crowded, lurching bus in Bangalore, would wrap itself around the handlebar like a snake and prevent him from falling on the horny hostel girl standing to his left.

He wakes up with the sun on his face. The orange of last night has been replaced with a different kind—less dense, more diffused.

He sits on the pot and drops his load. He sits with his elbows on his thighs. When he's finished he raises the seat, clambers onto the porcelain bowl and sits on it on his haunches. He washes himself listlessly. While getting off, his right toe loses its hold on the edge and he slips and falls on his right shoulder.

He doesn't bathe or brush his teeth. He wets his hair, combs it with his fingers. He changes into a blue, collared T-shirt and a pair of black jeans.

His dormitory is in Astley Hall. He decides to walk towards the clock tower. He hopes he does not bump into his mother on the way. The streets are full of people but Ravi finds it difficult to focus. He walks past a music store, a petrol station, a small Benetton's, two off-licences, and spare parts shops and jewellery stores, sitting cheek by jowl. The watch at the clock tower has the wrong time. He stands at the crossroads and thinks of the next step. Should he turn left and walk towards Imamullah Building? Should he turn right and go towards Paltan Bazaar or even a little further towards Suicide Alley, past the twin cinema halls? To buy time he crosses the road and stands next to the multicoloured water fountain opposite the head post office.

A couple sits on a bench whispering intensely and hardly looking up. A few daily wage labourers sit around the clock tower waiting for work. A boy sits with his weighing machine on the pavement near the water fountain. Ravi hands him a rupee and stands on what looks like a calibrated tablet. He doesn't look at the needle but at his toenails. They need a trim.

Ravi stands leaning against a railing, watching the women walk by. They laugh, smile, make eyes at passers-by; they touch each other's elbows and share secrets. All in all they seem happier than the men.

Curiously, Ravi cannot see them as a whole. He notices individual parts—disembodied and in isolation; he takes in breasts, waists and stomachs; necks, backs and feet; navels, lips and ears; elbows, cheekbones and ankles. He sees each part in its solitary grandeur or isolated ugliness. He sees each part for what it is.

He sees a group of three girls coming out of the Paltan Bazaar lane and crossing the road towards the post office. Hands, legs, necks. He sticks a clammy hand into his pocket and finds a piece of paper and a pen. His heart thuds hard against his chest, then sinks to his uncut toenails.

He walks up to the women and says, 'Excuse me, ma'am, I'm really sorry to bother you but I'm from Lakmé Cosmetics. We are doing a market survey on nail po . . .'

The girls haven't stopped walking. Ravi runs along with the scrap of paper in his hand, trying to stay abreast. One of the girls smiles at him, points at her watch and shakes her head.

'It's okay, ma'am,' says Ravi, getting the message and falling behind.

Another two girls pass; Ravi starts again, 'Excuse me ma'am, I'm really sorry to bother you but I'm from Lakmé Cosmetics. We are doing a market survey on nail polish. Would you like to answer a few questions? It won't take more than two minutes. Please ma'am, we have to do two hundred and fifty forms today.'

The girls stop. They are of college-going age. No, they

reply, of course they wouldn't mind answering a couple of questions. Ravi goes blank for a couple of seconds. He doesn't have any questions. He pretends to read from the scrap of paper in his hand.

'Ma'am, do you apply nail polish?'

'Yes.'

'Yes.'

'Ma'am, what's your favourite colour?'

'Metallic blue.'

'Silver.'

'Ma'am, what's your favourite company?'

'Revlon.'

'Avon.'

'Ma'am, do you like wearing your nails long or short?'

'Main to medium *rakhti hoon.'*

'Sirf special occasion *ke liye badha leti hoon.'*

The girls giggle individually while answering the questions, then they look at each other and giggle some more.

'Thank you ma'am,' says Ravi, 'that will be all.'

'That's it! *Bas?'* They sound disappointed. Ravi looks apologetic.

By now his heart is back in its rightful place and thudding really very hard. He looks at his crotch and immediately regrets not wearing underwear. He has a hard on. The bulge is visible. It's a big cock, not willing to go down without its moment in the sun.

Ravi takes out a handkerchief and wipes his face. His lips are dry and particled with chapped, dead skin. He looks around to see if anyone has seen him approach the passing girls. A couple of vendors seem to be looking at him but he can't tell for sure.

A girl dressed in sleeveless yellow salwar kameez passes by. She wears her hair loose, long, parted at the centre. She is slightly taller than him. Something catches the sun and glints in his eye. It's a thin silver bracelet on her left wrist. He stares at her long slender fingers and mauve fingernails. His feet begin to move. He follows faithfully, without volition, his eyes glued to her wrist, her silver bracelet.

They pass two cinema halls—the girl in front, Ravi on her heels, sometimes getting suspiciously close, then falling back, the braceletted wrist pulling him like a kinky magnet. He wants to kiss her there—just where the silver stops and her hands fall away into graceful, languid elegance.

The girl turns around twice and scowls but Ravi doesn't notice. His eyes are transfixed on that one shiny spot on her body. She begins to walk quickly, weaving in and out of the crowd, and on reaching Suicide Alley turns into a side lane.

A procession of cows forces Ravi onto a narrow cement platform on the side of the road. A burning rubbish mound, right behind where he stands, makes his eyes water. He is on the verge of tears; he knows he has lost her.

He gets back on the main road and walks towards Bindal Bridge, past the cane furniture shops and photo studios. The light in the sky has turned a dark grey, a moist cold wind whips him around the face. It's going to rain. Ravi keeps walking, without getting tired, without feeling anything. He is convinced that if he stops he will die. While crossing Bindal Bridge he realizes that the two girls walking in front of him are actually running away from him and that the cellphone in his hand is actually a piece of ripped cellophane.

He stops and turns back. 'Better mail Ma,' he mutters to himself.

Freshers' Welcome

'Let's go,' said Chandy, pulling on a pair of jeans. 'Grewal wanted us in his room at ten. We're running late.'

Everything about Chandy, my roommate, was boring: his face, his haircut, his taste in music. And he was really enthu about getting ragged which just added to his boringness.

Grewal's room—packed to capacity with seniors and freshers—resembled a strip bar. It was noisy and smoky. Juniors squatted on beer bottles in their birthday suits. Seeing so many people I said to Chandy, 'Let's go back, man. No one's gonna miss us.' But Chandy was adamant. He wanted to be grilled in the nude. He should have been in the army.

Ragging season was in full swing. In the past few days, I had been made to do strange things. It didn't help that I was perceived as a cocky fresher. I gave clever answers while maintaining an indifferent and dull visage. This mixture of cockiness and indifference riled the seniors no end. Word was out that Jha had to be broken.

I think I also got it bad because I had a big dick. Men with small cocks do not take nicely to those with big ones. Stripping neutralized the power equations: senior makes junior strip in order to humiliate him; junior's big cock makes senior feel pathetic about his dinky manhood.

Personally, I didn't mind stripping because I came from a boys' school where we jerked off in full view of each other. I didn't mind being made to run around the field at two in the morning, butt-naked in the pouring rain. Afterwards, one's dick hurt a little from being slapped around the thighs but it was okay.

It was the other, more tedious stuff that I hated. Like measuring the distance from the hostel to the main gate with a 12-inch scale. Or sitting on one's haunches and barking like a dog. Or humping a tree or pole dancing or washing underwear or crawling on all fours down a hostel corridor.

After half an hour, the room started emptying out. In the meanwhile, three more seniors had invited us to their rooms. I made a quick mental calculation: a minimum of fifty minutes in each room took us to four in the morning. This meant one more night without sleep.

Grewal was on the college soccer team. He always wore the same outfit: red baseball cap, tight black jeans, tight white T-shirt and dark brown Woodlands boots with extra-long laces. He never smiled and had the reputation of being a vicious ragger. We spent many hours strategizing: 'Thing with Grewal is—don't ever let on that he's got you bugged, else he's gonna fuck your happiness, man.' He also had the reputation of being a ladies' man. He was seen with a different girl at different times of the day. No wonder the juniors regarded him with a mixture of awe and fear and pointed him out to each other.

There were five of us in the room: Chandy, me and three other blokes. Grewal asked me to shut the door. He made everybody line up and stand at attention. He asked us to rattle off our personal details: name, city, school, the course we had enrolled for. We were ordered to suffix each answer with the word 'sir'. Before we could begin, there was a knock on the door. More seniors. The numbers were more or less equal now: four seniors and five juniors.

'Alex Chandy, sir. Kottayam, sir. Corpus Christi School, sir. Chemistry honours, sir.'

'Sumit Patel, sir. Ahmedabad, sir. K.V., sir. History, sir.'

'Mayank Agarwal, sir. La Marts, Lucknow, sir. Physics honours, sir.'

'Pratap Goswami, sir. Patna, sir. St. Xavier's, sir. BSc Computers, sir.'

Pradeep Jha, sir. Benares, sir. St. Paul's, sir. English honours, sir.'

The seniors found our answers extremely amusing. I knew from past experience not to smile at all. Humour was a privilege of the seniors, not to be encroached upon until given permission to do so. Sumit Patel had joined late and this was his first night in the hostel. When the seniors laughed at the way he pronounced 'Ahmedabad' he smiled nervously. Grewal bore down on him immediately: 'Wipe that smile off your face, you little shit. Now.'

Patel stopped smiling. Beads of perspiration appeared on his brow. Grewal turned to me and said, 'Tell this idiot how to do it properly.' I showed Patel how to form a pair of imaginary scissors using the middle and forefinger of his right hand, then snip his lips, grimacing visibly while doing so. Finally, the offending smile—now trapped in a clenched fist—had to be shoved up one's backside. Patel had to clip and shove again and again, until the seniors were satisfied.

Next, Grewal and his cronies asked us to strip. Chandy, Agarwal, Goswami and I were familiar with the ritual and went through the motions mechanically. Patel refused. He seemed livid at the suggestion.

Picking up a hockey stick lying in a corner of the room, Grewal walked up to Patel. Placing the stick horizontally across his neck, he pressed down on his Adam's apple until Patel began gasping for breath. 'You will do whatever I tell you to do. Get it?' Patel managed a weak 'yes'. This made Grewal even angrier. He muttered, 'Yes, *sir*. You will always address me, or any other senior for that matter, as "sir". Get it?'

'Yes, sir.'

'I can't hear you asshole.'

'YES, SIR.'

'Do what I tell you or I'll make Delhi University living hell for you. Get it?'

'YES, SIR.'

Grewal came back to his chair. Patel took his clothes off. Grewal turned to his cronies for ideas: 'What should we do with these stick insects?' They came up with suggestions: a dog race, ballroom dancing, a bodybuilding competition. Grewal didn't like any. 'What about a human train?' he offered, sounding excited. The cronies seconded the proposal. Within minutes, the five of us were chugging round the room, each bogey holding the penis of the bogey behind. Patel, the steam engine, was at the head of the train, holding his palm to his nose, the curve between his forefinger and thumb pressed vertically against his pouting lips, the thumb tucked under his chin. When Grewal wanted the train to go faster, he used his hockey stick to whack Chandy—the guard van—across the buttocks.

I met Feroz while having dinner in the college mess. We happened to be sitting next to each other. He asked me my name. I replied adding the mandatory 'sir' to the answer. He immediately asked me not to do so. He said he didn't believe in ragging juniors, and found the whole thing absurd and unnecessary.

Feroz was from an army background and had spent several years in a Simla boarding school. He was clean-shaven and soft-spoken. A delicate chin underlined his intelligent, inquisitive eyes. He spoke so softly one had to strain one's ears to hear him. He also displayed a childlike propensity to burst into giggles at the oddest of times. When I gave him my full name he wondered if I was related to a famous historian. I said I happened to be his son. Feroz smiled.

He wanted to know if the ragging had been bad. I said something non-committal like 'Yeah. It's okay.' He said he had heard that things were pretty awful in college this year. 'It's all right. I come from a pretty rough boys' school—I can take care of myself.'

'And anyway,' Feroz said, pointing out the light at the end of the tunnel, 'the Freshers' Welcome is less than a month away. Things will settle down after that.'

After dinner Feroz invited me to his room. We walked through the crowded main corridor—the nightly slave market—where unsuspecting juniors were picked up by seniors for next to nothing. I was grateful for Feroz's company. When the slave lords called out to me, he asked them to stay away.

Feroz was studying for a master's degree in a pre-dominantly undergraduate college. He had completed his bachelor's here and then decided to stay on. He liked the college that much. He was a historian, which is how he had heard of my father.

As a MA student, Feroz had been allotted a large room. From my first-year perspective, it looked fancy and luxurious. Such a big room and all to oneself! I suddenly wished I was older.

Most undergraduates decorated their walls with pictures of models ripped from foreign fashion magazines. In contrast, the walls of Feroz's room were bare. In fact, the entire room was bare except for the basic furniture provided by the college. He had pushed his writing desk and chair into an alcove in a far corner of the room. He found nice views a distraction when working. He said he didn't buy many books; most of the titles in the built-in bookshelf were from libraries: the British Council, the Max Mueller Bhavan and the Arts Faculty. From his books it was evident that Feroz read little else apart from his subject. There was hardly any poetry or fiction, except for a Ghalib translation and a volume of Manto's stories.

His place probably looked larger than it actually was for

another reason: Feroz had moved the string cot—given to every student by the college—out into the corridor. In its place he had kept a thick mattress under the only window in the room. By day it served as a sitting area for guests; at night he removed the bolsters and cushions and slept on it.

Feroz asked me to sit wherever I felt like: on the mattress or in the lone armchair the room possessed. I opted for the chair since I was wearing shoes and didn't plan on staying too long. We didn't speak much that first night. Feroz had a tutorial essay to complete. He asked me to stay for as long as I felt like. He said he was going to be up till very late. After several nights of ragging, I was grateful for the breathing space, this quiet little clearing which I had stumbled upon in the hostel jungle.

After that day, I went to Feroz's room often. We'd walk back together after dinner so that I didn't get caught by the seniors. He obviously liked working at night. I'd sit in the armchair listening to Blind Melon on my Walkman and reading a book. I made sure I went back when the most hardened raggers had gone to sleep. Feroz showed me a shortcut to the Ridge through the main university buildings. In the afternoons, I would slip away and walk around the wooded forest. At times I felt terribly homesick but always resisted the temptation to catch a train and go home.

There was resentment all around that Feroz took me to his room every day. On our walks back after dinner, I'd often catch a glimpse of a smirking senior, or a batchmate looking at me with superior, mocking eyes. But even a jungle spawns its own laws. One senior could not question the actions of another. Besides, I had been ragged by almost everybody.

These were really the last twenty days or so before the initiation period officially ended.

There were days when Feroz worked in complete silence and we didn't exchange a word. On other days he'd do nothing but talk. His army dad had wanted his son to follow in his footsteps and was greatly upset when Feroz decided to pursue history for a career. He seemed closer to his mother and spoke of her fondly. While growing up, he'd miss her terribly each time he went back to boarding school. He spoke of lying in his dorm bed and craving her softness, her perfumed chiffon saris, her cool white arms.

Being a historian, Feroz loved Delhi. On weekend afternoons, he'd disappear with one of his many girlfriends into the bylanes of Old Delhi. He would return in the evening, just before dinner, and speak excitedly about his discoveries: an engraving he had never seen before or an architectural feature he'd failed to spot on an earlier visit.

Girls loved Feroz. They didn't seem to mind when he touched their shoulders or put his arms around their waists. They pulled his leg, asked him for help when they didn't understand passages in books, tended to him when he fell sick. As far as I could tell, he knew all of them, was extremely close to some, but wasn't seeing anyone. Unlike him, I was very awkward and shy with women.

Once when he opened his cupboard, I was surprised to see pictures of Aishwarya Rai on the insides of the panels. She had recently won the Miss World pageant and was on the covers of various magazines. Feroz had carefully chosen close-ups of her face. He was a little embarrassed at having his little secret revealed but laughed it off saying, 'Being a serious MA student I can't possibly stick these pictures on my wall like some first-year public-school kid, can I?'

The day before Freshers' Welcome, Chandy and I found ourselves wandering the hostel corridors, looking for old clothes. We needed them because the ritual involved seniors throwing rotten tomatoes and eggs at juniors. We were not allowed to bring our own arsenal but we could, if we wanted, pick up what was thrown at us and hurl it back. Chandy was looking forward to the tamasha. He had greatly enjoyed getting ragged and seemed a little sad that the tomfoolery was finally coming to an end.

We had both arrived in college with new suitcases and new clothes. There was nothing in our wardrobes that was disposable. We went to Kamla Nagar Market looking for cheap T-shirts and shorts. Chandy and I had not spoken to each other much ever since I befriended Feroz. Sometimes I got the feeling that he was avoiding me. While walking to the market I raised the issue with him. He said, 'Why are you so thick with Feroz? You've almost disappeared from the scene, man!' I said I didn't really know how friendships began but I enjoyed his company. I didn't tell him that I was tired of the ragging and Feroz's room afforded me protection and privacy—two things I was extremely grateful for. Unlike Chandy, who thrived in a crowd, I treasured my space.

Chandy had a suspicious look on his face but didn't say anything. Instead, he tipped his head backwards and examined the overcast sky, 'I hope it rains tomorrow. It's going to be so much fun: eggs, tomatoes, pouring rain . . .' I pretended to agree. To convince him of my laddish abilities I walked into a grocery store and bought half a dozen eggs. 'I know it's not allowed but who cares? I'm carrying these with me tomorrow. I want to whack some guys too,' I said, trying to sound upbeat and combative.

Chandy cheered up visibly after my statement. He too decided to buy some eggs. 'Who do you want to get tomorrow?'

'Grewal. I hope to land at least one of these on his face.'

That night I went to Feroz's room as usual. I read the newspaper while Feroz worked at his desk. While I was there it began to rain. It looked like it wasn't going to stop all night. There was no way I was going to make it back to my block without getting completely drenched. I was also very tired. Feroz said, 'Why don't you crash here tonight?' I preferred waking up in my own bed but that didn't seem like a viable option tonight. I decided to stay. The mattress was really meant for one person so we decided to rest our heads on opposite sides. This way Feroz could smell my toes and I his: better than breathing into each other's faces.

At 2.30 in the afternoon, the Common Room lawns resembled a battleground. The seniors stood on a raised platform and surveyed the sea of juniors on the lawns below. At the given signal, everyone went hammer and tongs at each other. In the melee I couldn't see Grewal. The seniors were in a position of advantage. They were at a higher level and had pillars to hide behind; we, on the other hand, were completely exposed. In the end I didn't throw any eggs. I just stood there and took the punishment. War cries rent the air; boys stumbled and fell over each other. I caught a glimpse of Chandy howling pleasurably, egg yolk dripping from his forehead. Twenty minutes later a shrill whistle called a halt to the induced savagery. Seniors and juniors hugged each other. The boys had finally become men.

'So how was it?' asked Feroz. 'You are quite brave really. I ran away in my first year. Went to my local guardian's.'

'How did you manage that? Didn't they screw you later? Seniors came around to our rooms in the morning and warned us that if anyone went missing they'd make sure he got hell later on.'

Feroz said I took things too seriously. 'Do you think anyone remembers? Do you think anyone can see anything in that confusion?'

'I suppose you are right,' I said, smelling my arm for eggs. 'Anyway, it's all done now. I am a bona fide member of this college.'

'And you're going to smell of eggs for a week,' joked Feroz.

Feroz went back to his desk as he often did. For all his disinterest in the army, he had an army man's discipline when it came to working.

I lay down on the mattress. I was even more tired today. Last night had been uncomfortable with two grown men sharing a mattress meant for one.

I must have gone to sleep listening to my Walkman because when I opened my eyes I found Feroz lying next to me. He had somehow managed to squeeze into the narrow space between the wall and me. I felt sorry for him. Last night must have been uncomfortable for him too. I gave myself five minutes. Then I'd be off: rain or no rain.

I removed the Walkman from my chest and put it on the floor. I was about to get up when Feroz's heavy head lolled onto my chest. For a second, I was startled. I was reminded of chair-car journeys where one often wakes up to find a fellow passenger's head on one's shoulder.

I was wondering how to extricate myself from the situation without waking Feroz up when he opened his big, black, mournful eyes. We remained like that for a few seconds, observing each other from up close. I felt his breath on mine and it felt nice. Soon he was straddling me, squeezing my behind, exploring my mouth with his pink tongue. I had never been kissed before. I had a massive boner. I didn't protest when Feroz untied my pyjama strings and jerked me off with a sure and practiced hand.

We extricated ourselves from each other in silence. He said he was going to the toilet to wash up. I left the room before he could return. I walked very slowly. I was euphoric, yet frightened. I didn't feel like laughing or crying or angry or anything. I kept telling myself, 'Pradeep, you are not gay.'

It was about two in the morning. I saw three boys walking in my direction. On coming closer, I recognized one of them as Grewal. We didn't greet each other. But as they were passing me, Grewal turned around and said something. I think he said 'Fucking faggot' but it's quite possible that I misheard him. It could be he just said 'Hello Pradeep.'

Acknowledgements

'The Other Evening' appeared in *First Proof 1: The Penguin Book of New Writing in India* (Penguin Books), and 'The Farewell' (as 'Sex and the Small Town') in *The Last Bungalow: Writings on Allahabad* (Penguin Books) and *Brick* (Canada). Grateful acknowledgement is made to the editors.

Read more in Penguin

THE WOMEN IN CAGES: COLLECTED STORIES
Vilas Sarang

With his debut collection of short stories in English, *Fair Tree of the Void* (1990), Vilas Sarang established himself as a writer of great gifts, and one with a unique sensibility and literary vision. His works since—in Marathi and English—have confirmed his reputation as one of India's finest and most daring contemporary writers.

The Women in Cages brings together all his short stories written in English, both previously published and new, brilliantly highlighting his singular imagination and style. From the desecration of a funeral pyre by the simple act of warming one's hands on the blaze to the transformation of a man into a gigantic phallus enticing crowds of devotees as a live symbol of Lord Shiva; from the prostitute who uses the occult to generate numerous vaginas all over her body to a military general who abolishes an entire season for fear of revolution, Sarang presents startling thematic variety, always suggestive of strange and haunting alternative universes that transcend time and space.

Gritty and disturbing, and leavened by wit and compassion, *The Women in Cages* is a masterful attempt at capturing the myriad nuances of modern life.

'One of the finest Indian writers of his time'—Dom Moraes

'Sarang is an original: he writes clearly and beautifully about often bizarre events in a precisely realized world'—Anthony Thwaite, poet and former editor of *Encounter*

Fiction
Rs 275

Read more in Penguin

ELVIS, RAJA: STORIES

M.G. Vassanji

With the assurance, the mastery of vivid detail, and the ear for the nuances of the voice that have garnered him such admiration, Vassanji weaves twelve haunting tales of lives transplanted, of the traumas small and large of migration, of the bitterness of memory and the unexpected consequences of hope.

Meeting his college friend Rusty after years, Diamond is faced once again with a past he had chosen to outgrow and forget. Haunted by the memory of his wife's betrayal, he finds himself trapped in Rusty's world, his shrine to Elvis. As he struggles to escape from this unnatural prison, Diamond finds help from an unexpected ally . . . In 'When She Was Queen' a young man questions his mother about a rumour that has circulated amongst his older siblings for years: that their father once lost their mother in a poker game. According to the rumour, their mother spent a night in the bed of a local magnate. In his quest to comprehend the implications of this rumour, the narrator uncovers an even darker secret. A young African-born Indian visits his ancestral village in drought-stricken Gujarat in search of a wife, and discovers instead an unexpected destiny in 'The Expected One'.

Negotiating between her past and her present in 'Her Two Husbands', the widow of a university professor finds herself increasingly a prisoner of the edicts of her new husband's spiritual advisor. On Halloween night an insulted man lays bare his horrifying plan of revenge in 'Is It Still October'. And in 'She, with Bill and George' a young Indian woman forms unlikely bonds with two men—one American, the other Masai—in 1970s Tanzania that reverberate through her life.

Quiet and composed, penetrating and startling, *Elvis, Raja: Stories* is a portrait of an increasingly modern condition, of lives caught in our swiftly changing, often contradictory world.

'The kind of sweeping, multilayered, turbulent narrative of near-hallucinatory power that is the hallmark of Vassanji's best work'—*The Globe and Mail*

Fiction
Rs 250

THE LAST DRAGON DANCE: CHINATOWN STORIES
Kwai-yun Li

On a hot summer day in 1942, sitting outside her shoe shop in Bentinck Street, a mother fixes her six-year-old daughter's marriage to her neighbour's son. A widow converts a part of her house to a temple so that she can support her family with the donations.

During a border skirmish in the north-east, Chinese mothers prepare packages for life in concentration camps giving special instructions to the children, lest they get separated. A gentle bookseller and his daughter disappear in the middle of the night when they are deported to China for his political sympathies.

And in the delightful story 'Uncle Worry', Uncle Chien worries when his daughter Pi Moi forgets to call him: he worries that she and her husband, Mohamed, have had a falling out. He worries when Pi Moi does call, for she must be fighting with Mohamed, otherwise why would she call?

From crumbling shops in Chinatown to decaying tanneries in Tangra, Kwai-Yun Li's *The Last Dragon Dance: Chinatown Stories*, exposes us to the life of the little-known Chinese community in Calcutta. While the arrival of the Chinese in India abounds in legends, the mass exodus of this dwindling community is not as romantic: political and economic upheavals have forced them to abandon their home.

Even though theirs is so much a story of assimilation and syncretism—growing up in 1950s' Calcutta one never paid much attention to which customs were Indian or Chinese—the Chinese have often felt the brunt of their foreignness. The rift between Mao and Chiang Kai Shek led to the deportment and imprisonment of hundreds of Maoist sympathizers.

This collection gives voice to such concerns without being overtly sentimental or sensational; Li never fails to see the humour in the idiosyncrasies of her community. These inspired-from-life stories wonderfully capture the mood of the time with unassuming grace.

'Kwai-Yun Li's debut collection . . . about being Chinese in 1950s India, proves her a natural story-teller'—*Tehelka*

Fiction
Rs 199

NEXT DOOR: STORIES

Jahnavi Barua

In eleven superbly crafted stories Jahnavi Barua takes us into the private, individual worlds of a varied cast of characters and exposes the intricate mesh of emotions so often concealed under the façade of everyday lives. Innocent desires and furtive longings, the complexity of fierce love and the terrible consequences of its betrayal, simple aspirations that compel brave action, life's startling reversals that reveal deep insecurities and yet pave the way for forgiveness and reconciliation—these are just some of the themes played out in these remarkably nuanced snapshots of life. Predominantly set in the verdant, politically charged landscape of Assam, yet constantly transcending the particular, the stories in Next Door are unerringly human. Subtle and evocative in their telling, they mark the introduction of a highly accomplished voice.

'Filled with deft descriptions, wrenching surprises and a deep understanding of what it means to be human, this first collection by Jahnavi Barua is worthy of a careful read'—Chitra Lekha Banerjee Divakaruni

'Like the Brahmaputra, Jahnavi Barua's stories are rich, full and flow with ease, with sudden startling glimpses of turbulence under the placid surface. A powerful and confident voice' —Shashi Deshpande

'Jahnavi Barua's stories are charged with affection for a landscape and an understanding of how it enters the human patterns of loving and living. A wonderful and moving book'—Anjum Hasan

Fiction
Rs 250